The *VOYAGES* of
DOCTOR DOLITTLE

The VOYAGES of
DOCTOR DOLITTLE

ILLUSTRATED BY THE AUTHOR

BY HUGH LOFTING

RED FOX

A Red Fox Book

Published by Random House Children's Books
20 Vauxhall Bridge Road, London SW1V 2SA

A division of Random House UK Limited

London Melbourne Sydney Auckland
Johannesburg and agencies throughout the world

First published in Great Britain by Jonathan Cape Ltd 1923
Red Fox revised edition 1991

3 5 7 9 10 8 6 4

T!
sl
re
tł
bi

p'
in

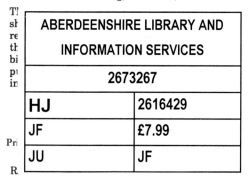
Pri

R.

Papers used by Random House UK Limited
are natural, recyclable products made from wood grown in
sustainable forests. The manufacturing processes conform to
the environmental regulations of the country of origin.

ISBN 0 09 985470 8

TO
COLIN AND ELIZABETH

'It's a letter,' he said – 'a picture letter. All these little things put together mean a message. But why give a message to a beetle to carry – and to a jabizri, the rarest beetle in the world? What an extraordinary thing!'

Then he fell to muttering over the pictures.

'I wonder what it means: men walking up a mountain; men walking into a hole in a mountain; a mountain falling down – it's a good drawing, that; men pointing to their open mouths; bars – prison bars, perhaps; men praying; men lying down – they look as though they might be sick; and, last of all, just a mountain – a peculiar-shaped mountain.'

All of a sudden the Doctor looked up sharply at me, a wonderful smile of delighted understanding spreading over his face.

'*Long Arrow!*' he cried. 'Don't you see, Stubbins? Why, of course! Only a naturalist would think of doing a thing like this: giving his letter to a beetle – not to a common beetle, but to the rarest of all, one that other naturalists would try to catch. Well, well! Long Arrow! A picture-letter from Long Arrow. For pictures are the only writing that he knows.'

'Yes, but who is the letter to?' I asked.

'It's to me, very likely. Miranda had told him, I know, years ago, that some day I meant to come here. But if not for me then it's for anyone who caught the beetle and read it. It's a letter to the world.'

'Well, but what does it say? It doesn't seem to me that it's much good to you now you've got it.'

'Yes, it is,' he said, 'because, look, I can read it now. First picture: men walking up a mountain – that's Long Arrow and his party; men going into a hole in a mountain – they enter a cave looking for medicine plants or mosses; a mountain falling down – some hanging rocks must have slipped and trapped them, imprisoned them in the cave. And this was the only living creature that could carry a message for them to the outside world – a beetle, who could *burrow* his way into the open air. Of course it was only a slim chance that the beetle would ever be caught and the letter read. But it *was* a chance, and when men are in great danger they grab at any straw of hope. . . . All right, now look at the next picture: men pointing to their open mouths – they are hungry; men praying – begging anyone who finds this letter to come to their assistance; men lying down – they are sick or starving. This letter, Stubbins, is their last cry for help.'

He sprang to his feet as he ended, snatched out a notebook, and put the letter between the leaves. His hands were trembling with haste and agitation.

'Come on!' he cried. 'Up the mountain – all of you. There's not a moment to lose. Bumpo, bring the water and nuts with you. Heavens only knows how long they've been pining underground. Let's hope and pray we're not too late!'

'But were are you going to look?' I asked. 'Miranda said the island was a hundred miles long and the mountains seem to run all the way down the centre of it.'

'Didn't you see the last picture?' he said, grabbing up his hat from the ground and cramming it on his head. 'It was an oddly shaped mountain – looked like a hawk's head. Well, there's where he is – if he's still alive. First thing for us to do is to get up on a high peak and look around the island for a mountain shaped like a hawk's head. Just

Just to think of it! There's a chance of my meeting Long Arrow, the son of Golden Arrow, after all! Come on! Hurry! To delay may mean death to the greatest naturalist ever born!'

Chapter Seven
HAWK'S-HEAD MOUNTAIN

W E all agreed afterwards that none of us had ever worked so hard in our lives before as we did that day. For my part, I know I was often on the point of dropping exhausted with fatigue; but I just kept on going – like a machine – determined that, whatever happened, *I* would not be the first to give up.

When we had scrambled to the top of a high peak, almost instantly we saw the strange mountain pictured in the letter. In shape it was the perfect image of a hawk's head and was, as far as we could see, the second highest summit on the island.

Although we were all out of breath from our climb, the Doctor didn't let us rest a second as soon as he had sighted it. With one look at the sun for direction, down he dashed again, breaking through thickets, splashing over brooks, taking all the short cuts. For a fat man, he was certainly the swiftest cross-country runner I ever saw.

We floundered after him as fast as we could. When I say *we*, I mean Bumpo and myself; for the animals, Jip, Chee-Chee, and Polynesia, were a long way ahead – even beyond the Doctor – enjoying the hunt like a paper-chase.

At length we arrived at the foot of the mountain we were making for, and we found its sides very steep. Said the Doctor, 'Now we will separate and search for caves. This spot where we now are will be our meeting place. If anyone finds anything like a cave or a hole where the earth and rocks have fallen in, he must shout and hulloa to the rest of us. If we find nothing we will all gather here in about an hour's time. Everybody understand?'

Then we all went off our different ways.

Each of us, you may be sure, was anxious to be the one to make a discovery. And never was a mountain searched so thoroughly. But alas! nothing could we find that looked in the least like a fallen-in cave. There were plenty of places where rocks had tumbled down to the foot of the slopes, but none of these appeared as though caves or passages could possibly lie behind them.

One by one, tired and disappointed, we straggled back to the meeting place. The Doctor seemed gloomy and impatient but by no means inclined to give up.

'Jip,' he said, 'couldn't you *smell* any men hiding anywhere?'

'No,' said Jip. 'I sniffed at every crack on the mountainside. But I am afraid my nose will be of no use to you here, Doctor. The trouble is, the whole air is so saturated with the smell of spider monkeys that it drowns every other scent. And besides, it's too cold and dry for good smelling.'

'It is certainly that,' said the Doctor, 'and getting colder all the time. I'm afraid the island is still drifting southward. Let's hope it stops before long or we won't be able to get even nuts and fruit to eat. Everything on the island will perish. Chee-Chee, what luck did you have?'

'None, Doctor. I climbed to every peak and pinnacle I could see. I searched every hollow and cleft. But not one place could I find where men might be hidden.'

'And Polynesia,' asked the Doctor, 'did you see nothing that might put us on the right track?'

'Not a thing, Doctor, but I have a plan.'

'Oh, good!' cried John Dolittle, full of hope renewed. 'What is it? Let's hear it.'

'You still have that beetle with you,' she asked – 'the biz-biz, or whatever it is you call the wretched insect?'

'Yes,' said the Doctor, producing the glass-topped box from his pocket, 'here it is.'

'All right. Now, listen,' said she. 'If what you have supposed is true – that is, that Long Arrow had been trapped inside the mountain by falling rock, he probably found that beetle inside the cave – perhaps many other different beetles too, eh? He wouldn't have been likely to take the biz-biz in with him, would he? He was hunting plants, you say, not beetles. Isn't that right?'

'Yes,' said the Doctor, 'that's probably so.'

'Very well. It is fair to suppose then that the beetle's home, or his hole, is in that place – the part of the mountain where Long Arrow and his party are imprisoned, isn't it?'

'Quite, quite.'

'All right. Then the thing to do is to let the

beetle go – and watch him; and sooner or later he'll return to his home in Long Arrow's cave. And there we will follow him. Or at all events,' she added smoothing down her wing feathers with a very superior air, 'we will follow him till the miserable bug starts nosing under the earth. But at least he will show us what part of the mountain Long Arrow is hidden in.'

'But he may fly, if I let him out,' said the Doctor. 'Then we shall just lose him and be no better off than we were before.'

'*Let* him fly,' snorted Polynesia scornfully. 'A parrot can wing it as fast as a biz-biz, I fancy. If he takes to the air, I'll guarantee not to let the little devil out of my sight. And if he just crawls along the ground you can follow him yourself.'

'Splendid!' cried the Doctor. 'Polynesia, you have a great brain. I'll set him to work at once and see what happens.'

Again we all clustered around the Doctor as he carefully lifted off the glass lid and let the big beetle climb out upon his finger.

'Ladybug, ladybug, fly away home!' crooned Bumpo. 'Your house is on fire and your chil—'

'Oh, do be quiet!' snapped Polynesia crossly.

'Stop insulting him! Don't you suppose he has wits enough to go home without your telling him?'

'I thought perchance he might be of a philandering disposition,' said Bumpo humbly. 'It could be that he is tired of his home and needs to be encouraged. Shall I sing him "Home, Sweet Home," think you?'

'No. Then he'd never go back. Your voice needs a rest. Don't sing to him: just watch him. . . . Oh, and Doctor, why not tie another message to the creature's leg, telling Long Arrow that we're doing our best to reach him and that he mustn't give up hope?'

'I will,' said the Doctor. And in a minute he had pulled a dry leaf from a bush nearby and was covering it with little pictures in pencil.

At last, neatly fixed up with his new mailbag, Mr Jabizri crawled off the Doctor's finger to the ground and looked about him. He stretched his legs, polished his nose with his front feet, and then moved off leisurely to the west.

We had expected him to walk *up* the mountain; instead, he walked *around* it. Do you know how long it takes a beetle to walk around a mountain? Well, I assure you it takes an unbelievably long time. As the hours dragged by, we hoped and hoped that he would get up and fly the rest, and let Polynesia carry on the work of following him. But he never opened his wings once. I had not realized before how hard it is for a human being to walk slowly enough to keep up with a beetle. It was the most tedious thing I have ever gone through. And as we dawdled along behind, watching him like hawks lest we lose him under a leaf or something, we all got so cross and ill-tempered we were ready to bite one another's heads off. And when he stopped to look at the scenery or polish his nose some more, I could hear Polynesia behind me letting out the most dreadful swear words you ever heard.

After he had led us the whole way round the mountain he brought us to the exact spot where we started from and there he came to a dead stop.

'Well,' said Bumpo to Polynesia, 'what do you think of the beetle's sense now? You see he *doesn't* know enough to go home.'

'Oh, be still!' snapped Polynesia. 'Wouldn't *you* want to stretch your legs for exercise if you'd been shut up in a box all day? Probably his home is near here, and that's why he's come back.'

'But why,' I asked, 'did he go the whole way round the mountain first?'

Then the three of us got into a violent argument. But in the middle of it all the Doctor suddenly called out, 'Look, look!'

We turned and found that he was pointing to the jabizri, who was now walking *up* the mountain at a much faster and more business-like gait.

'Well,' said Bumpo, sitting down wearily, 'if he is going to walk *over* the mountain and back for more exercise, I'll wait for him here. Chee-Chee and Polynesia can follow him.'

Indeed it would have taken a monkey or a bird to climb the place that the beetle was now walking up. It was a smooth, flat part of the mountain's side, steep as a wall.

But presently, when the jabizri was no more than ten feet above our heads, we all cried out together. For, even while we watched him, he had disappeared into the face of the rock like a raindrop soaking into sand.

'He's gone,' cried Polynesia. 'There must be a hole up there.' And in a twinkling she had fluttered up the rock and was clinging to the face of it with her claws.

'Yes,' she shouted down, 'we've run him to earth at last. His hole is right here, behind a patch of lichen, big enough to get two fingers in.'

'Ah,' cried the Doctor, 'this great slab of rock then must have slid down from the summit and shut off the mouth of the cave like a door. Poor fellows! What a dreadful time they must have spent in there! Oh, if we only had some picks and shovels now!'

'Picks and shovels wouldn't do much good,' said Polynesia. 'Look at the size of the slab: a hundred feet high and as many broad. You would need an army for a week to make any impression on it.'

'I wonder how thick it is,' said the Doctor, and he picked up a big stone and banged it with all his might against the face of the rock. It made a hollow booming sound, like a giant drum. We all stood still listening while the echo of it died slowly away.

And then a cold shiver ran down my spine. For, from within the mountain, back came three answering knocks: *Boom! . . . Boom! . . . Boom!*

Wide-eyed we looked at one another as though the earth itself had spoken. And the

'He banged it with all his might against the face of the rock'

solemn little silence that followed was broken by the Doctor.

'Thank heaven,' he said in a hushed reverent voice, 'some of them at least are alive!'

PART V

Chapter One
A GREAT MOMENT

THE next part of our problem was the hardest of all: how to roll aside, pull down, or break open that gigantic slab. As we gazed up at it towering above our heads, it looked indeed a hopeless task for our tiny strength.

But the sounds of life from inside the mountain had put new heart in us. And in a moment we were all scrambling around trying to find any opening or crevice that would give us something to work on. Chee-Chee scaled up the sheer wall of the slab and examined the top of it where it leaned against the mountain's side; I uprooted bushes and stripped off hanging creepers that might conceal a weak place; the Doctor got more leaves and composed new picture-letters for the jabizri to take in if he should turn up again; whilst Polynesia carried up a handful of nuts and pushed them through the beetle's hole, one by one, for the prisoners inside to eat.

'Nuts are so nourishing,' she said.

But Jip it was who, scratching at the foot of the slab like a good ratter, made the discovery which led to our final success.

'Doctor,' he cried, running up to John Dolittle with his nose all covered with black mud, 'this slab is resting on nothing but a bed of soft earth. You never saw such easy digging. I guess the cave behind must be just too high up for the Indians to reach the earth with their hands, or they could have scraped a way out long ago. If we can only scratch the earthbed away from under, the slab might drop a little. Then maybe the Indians can climb out over the top.'

The Doctor hurried to examine the place where Jip had dug.

'Why, yes,' he said, 'if we can get the earth away from under this front edge, the slab is standing up so straight, we might even make it fall right down in this direction. It's well worth trying. Let's get at it, quick.'

We had no tools but the sticks and slivers

of stone which we could find around. A strange sight we must have looked, the whole crew of us squatting down on our heels, scratching and burrowing at the foot of the mountain, like six badgers in a row.

After about an hour, during which in spite of the cold the sweat fell from our foreheads in all directions, the Doctor said, 'Be ready to jump from under, clear out of the way, if she shows signs of moving. If this slab falls on anybody, it will squash him flatter than a pancake.'

Presently there was a grating, grinding sound.

'Look out!' yelled John Dolittle. 'Here she comes! Scatter!'

We ran for our lives, outward, towards the sides. The big rock slid gently down about a foot, into the trough that we had made beneath it. For a moment I was disappointed, for like that, it was as hopeless as before – no signs of a cave mouth showing above it. But as I looked upward, I saw the top coming very slowly away from the mountainside. We had unbalanced it below. As it moved apart from the face of the mountain, sounds of human voices, crying gladly in a strange tongue, issued from behind.

Faster and faster the top swung forward, downward. Then, with a roaring crash that shook the whole mountain range beneath our feet, it struck the earth and cracked in halves.

How can I describe to anyone that first meeting between the two greatest naturalists the world ever knew, Long Arrow, the son of Golden Arrow and John Dolittle, M.D., of Puddleby-on-the-Marsh? The scene rises before me now, plain and clear in every detail, though it took place so many, many years ago. But when I come to write of it, words seem such poor things with which to tell you of that great occasion.

I know that the Doctor, whose life was surely full enough of big happenings, always counted the setting free of the Indian scientist as the greatest thing he ever did. For my part, knowing how much this meeting must mean to him, I was on pins and needles of expectation and curiosity as the great stone finally thundered down at our feet and we gazed across it to see what lay behind.

The gloomy black mouth of a tunnel, full twenty feet high, was revealed. In the centre of this opening stood an enormous

Indian, seven feet tall, handsome, muscular, slim, and naked but for a beaded cloth about his middle and an eagle's feather in his hair. He held one hand across his face to shield his eyes from the blinding sun, which he had not seen in many days.

'It is he!' I heard the Doctor whisper at my elbow. 'I know him by his great height and the scar upon his chin.'

And he stepped forward slowly across the fallen stone with his hand outstretched to the man.

Presently the Indian uncovered his eyes. And I saw that they had a curious piercing gleam in them – like the eyes of an eagle, but kinder and more gentle. He slowly raised his right arm, the rest of him still and motionless like a statue, and took the Doctor's hand in his. It was a great moment. Polynesia nodded to me in a knowing, satisfied kind of way. And I heard old Bumpo sniffle sentimentally.

Then the Doctor tried to speak to Long Arrow. But the Indian knew no English, of course, and the Doctor knew no Indian. Presently, to my surprise, I heard the Doctor trying him in different animal languages.

'It was a great moment'

'How do you do?' he said in dog talk; 'I am glad to see you,' in horse signs; 'How long have you been buried?' in deer language. Still the Indian made no move but stood there, straight and stiff, understanding not a word.

The Doctor tried again, in several other animal dialects. But with no result.

Till at last he came to the language of eagles.

'Great Long Arrow,' he said in the fierce screams and short grunts that the big birds use, 'never have I been so glad in all my life as I am today to find you still alive.'

In a flash Long Arrow's stony face lit up with a smile of understanding, and back came the answer in eagle tongue, 'Mighty Friend, I owe my life to you. For the remainder of my days I am your servant to command.'

Afterwards Long Arrow told us that this was the only bird or animal language that he had ever been able to learn. But that he had not spoken it in a long time, for no eagles ever came to this island.

Then the Doctor signalled to Bumpo, who came forward with the nuts and water. But Long Arrow neither ate nor drank. Taking the supplies with a nod of thanks, he turned and carried them into the inner dimness of the cave. We followed him.

Inside we found nine other Indians, men, women and boys, lying on the rock floor in a dreadful state of thinness and exhaustion.

Some had their eyes closed, as if dead. Quickly the Doctor went round them all and listened to their hearts. They were all alive, but one woman was too weak even to stand upon her feet.

At a word from the Doctor, Chee-Chee and Polynesia sped off into the jungle after more fruit and water.

While Long Arrow was handing round what food we had to his starving friends, we suddenly heard a sound outside the cave. Turning about we saw, clustered at the entrance, the band of Indians who had met us so inhospitably at the beach.

They peered into the dark cave cautiously at first. But as soon as they saw Long Arrow and the other Indians with us, they came rushing in, laughing, clapping their hands with joy, and jabbering away at a tremendous rate.

Long Arrow explained to the Doctor that the nine Indians we had found in the cave with him were two families who had accompanied him into the mountains to help him gather medicine plants. And while they had been searching for a kind of moss – good for indigestion – which grows only inside damp caves, the great rock slab had slid down and shut them in. Then for two weeks they had lived on the medicine moss and such fresh water as could be found dripping from the damp walls of the cave. The other Indians on the island had given them up for lost and mourned them as dead, and they were now very surprised and happy to find their relatives alive.

When Long Arrow turned to the newcomers and told them in their own language that it was this man who had found and freed their relatives, they gathered around John Dolittle, all talking at once and beating their breasts.

Long Arrow said they were apologizing and trying to tell the Doctor how sorry they were that they had seemed unfriendly to him at the beach. They had never seen a man like him before and had really been afraid of him – especially when they saw him conversing with the porpoises. They had thought he was the devil, they said.

Then they went outside and looked at the great stone we had thrown down, big as a meadow; and they walked round and round it, pointing to the break running through the middle and wondering how the trick of felling it was done.

Travellers who have since visited Spider Monkey Island tell me that that huge stone slab is now one of the regular sights of the island. And that the Indian guides, when showing it to visitors, always tell *their* story of how it came there. They say that when the Doctor found that the rocks had entrapped his friend, Long Arrow, he was so angry that he ripped the mountain in halves with his bare hands and let him out.

Chapter Two
'THE PEOPLE OF THE MOVING LAND'

FROM that time on the Indians' treatment of us was very different. We were invited to their village for a feast to celebrate the recovery of the lost families. And after we had made a litter from saplings to carry the sick woman in, we all started off down the mountain.

On the way the Indians told Long Arrow something which appeared to be sad news, for on hearing it, his face grew very grave. The Doctor asked him what was wrong. And Long Arrow said he had just been informed that the chief of the tribe, an old man of eighty, had died early that morning.

'That,' Polynesia whispered in my ear, 'must have been what they went back to the village for, when the messenger fetched them from the beach. Remember?'

'What did he die of?' asked the Doctor.

'He died of cold,' said Long Arrow.

Indeed, now that the sun was setting, we were all shivering ourselves.

'This is a serious thing,' said the Doctor to me. 'The island is still in the grip of that wretched current flowing southward. We will have to look into this tomorrow. If nothing can be done about it, the Indians had better take to canoes and leave the island. The chance of being wrecked will be better than getting frozen to death in the ice floes of the Antarctic.'

Presently we came over a saddle in the hills, and looking downward on the far side of the island, we saw the village – a large cluster of grass huts and gaily coloured totem poles close by the edge of the sea.

'How artistic!' said the Doctor. 'Delightfully situated. What is the name of the village?'

'Popsipetel,' said Long Arrow. 'That is the name also of the tribe. The word signifies in Indian tongue, *the people of the moving land*. There are two tribes of Indians on the island: the Popsipetels at this end and the Bag-jagderags at the other.'

'Which is the larger of the two peoples?'

'The Bag-jagderags, by far. Their city covers two square leagues. But,' added Long Arrow a slight frown darkening his handsome face, 'for me, I would rather have one Popsipetel than a hundred Bag-jagderags.'

The news of the rescue we had made had evidently gone ahead of us. For as we drew nearer to the village we saw crowds of Indians streaming out to greet the friends and relatives whom they had never thought to see again.

These good people, when they too were told how the rescue had been the work of the strange visitor to their shores, all gathered round the Doctor, shook him by the hands, patted him, and hugged him. Then they lifted him up upon their strong shoulders and carried him down the hill into the village.

There the welcome we received was even more wonderful. In spite of the cold air of the coming night, the villagers, who had all been shivering within their houses, threw open their doors and came out in hundreds. I had no idea that the little village could hold so many. They thronged about us, smiling and nodding and waving their hands; and as the details of what we had done were recited by

Long Arrow, they kept shouting strange singing noises, which we supposed were words of gratitude or praise.

We were next escorted to a brand-new grass house, clean and sweet-smelling within, and informed that it was ours. Six strong Indian boys were told to be our servants.

On our way through the village we noticed a house, larger than the rest, standing at the end of the main street. Long Arrow pointed to it and told us it was the Chief's house, but that it was now empty – no new chief having yet been elected to take the place of the old one who had died.

Inside our new home a feast of fish and fruit had been prepared. Most of the more important men of the tribe were already seating themselves at the long dining table when we got there. Long Arrow invited us to sit down and eat.

This we were glad enough to do, as we were all hungry. But we were both surprised and disappointed when we found that the fish had not been cooked. The Indians did not seem to think this extraordinary in the least, but went ahead gobbling the fish with much relish the way it was, raw.

With many apologies, the Doctor explained to Long Arrow that if they had no objection we would prefer our fish cooked.

Imagine our astonishment when we found that the great Long Arrow, so learned in the natural sciences, did not know what the word *cooked* meant!

Polynesia, who was sitting on the bench between John Dolittle and myself, pulled the Doctor by the sleeve.

'I'll tell you what's wrong, Doctor,' she whispered as he leant down to listen to her: *These people have no fires!* They don't know how to make a fire. Look outside: it's almost dark, and there isn't a light showing in the whole village. This is a fireless people.'

Chapter Three
FIRE

THEN the Doctor asked Long Arrow if he knew what fire was, explaining it to him by pictures drawn on the buckskin tablecloth. Long Arrow said he had seen such a thing coming out of the tops of volcanoes, but that neither he nor any of the Popsipetels knew how it was made.

'No wonder the old chief died of cold!' muttered Bumpo.

At that moment we heard a crying sound at the door. And turning round, we saw a weeping Indian mother with a baby in her arms. She said something to the Indians that we could not understand, and Long Arrow told us the baby was sick and she wanted the doctor to try and cure it.

'Oh, Lord!' groaned Polynesia in my ear.

'Just like Puddleby: patients arriving in the middle of dinner. Well, one thing, the food's raw so nothing can get cold anyway.'

The Doctor examined the baby and found at once that it was thoroughly chilled.

'Fire . . . *fire*! That's what it needs,' he said, turning to Long Arrow. 'That's what you all need. This child will have pneumonia if it isn't kept warm.'

'Aye, truly. But how to make a fire?' said Long Arrow. 'Where to get it? That is the difficulty. All the volcanoes in this land are dead.'

Then we fell to hunting through our pockets to see if any matches had survived the shipwreck. The best we could muster were two whole ones and a half – all with the heads soaked off them by salt water.

'Hark, Long Arrow,' said the Doctor, 'divers ways there be of making fire without the aid of matches. One: with a strong glass and the rays of the sun. That, however, since the sun has set, we cannot now employ. Another is by grinding a hard stick into a soft log. Is the daylight gone without? Alas, yes. Then I fear we must await the morrow, for besides the different woods, we need an old squirrel's nest for fuel. And that, without lamps, you could not find in your forests at this hour.'

'Great are your cunning and your skill, oh Great Doctor,' Long Arrow replied. 'But in this you do us an injustice. Know you not that all fireless people can see in the dark? Having no lamps we are forced to train ourselves to travel through the blackest night, lightless. I will dispatch a messenger and you shall have your squirrel's nest within the hour.'

He gave an order to two of our boy servants who promptly disappeared, running. And sure enough, in a very short space of time a squirrel's nest, together with hard and soft woods, was brought to our door.

The moon had not yet risen and within the house it was practically pitch-black. I could feel and hear, however, that the Indians were moving about comfortably as though it were daylight. The task of making fire the Doctor had to perform almost entirely by the sense of touch, asking Long Arrow and the Indians to hand him his tools when he mislaid them in the dark. And then I made a curious discovery: now that I had to, I found that I was beginning to see a little in the dark myself. And for the first time I realized that of course there *is* no such thing as pitch-dark, so long as you have a door open or a sky above you.

Calling for the loan of a bow, the Doctor loosened the string, put the hard stick into a loop, and began grinding this stick into the soft wood of the log. Soon I smelled that the log was smoking. Then he kept feeding the part that was smoking with the inside lining of the squirrel's nest, and he asked me to blow upon it with my breath. He made the stick drill faster and faster. More smoke filled the room. And at last the darkness about us was suddenly lit up. The squirrel's nest had burst into flame.

The Indians murmured and grunted with astonishment. At first they were all for falling on their knees and worshipping the fire. Then they wanted to pick it up with their bare hands and play with it. We had to teach them how it was to be used, and they were quite fascinated when we laid our fish across it on sticks and cooked it. They sniffed the air with relish as, for the first time in history, the smell of fried fish passed through the village of Popsipetel.

Then we got them to bring us piles and stacks of dry wood, and we made an enormous bonfire in the middle of the main street. Around this, when they felt its warmth, the whole tribe gathered and smiled and wondered. It was a striking sight, one of the pictures from our voyages that I most frequently remember: that roaring jolly blaze beneath the black night sky, and all about it a vast ring of Indians, the firelight gleaming on bronze cheeks, white teeth, and flashing eyes – a whole town trying to get warm, giggling and pushing like schoolchildren.

In a little, when we had got them more used to the handling of fire, the Doctor showed them how it could be taken into their houses if a hole were only made in the roof to let the smoke out. And before we turned in after that long, long, tiring day, we had fires going in every hut in the village.

The poor people were so glad to get really warm again that we thought they'd never go to bed. Well on into the early hours of the morning the little town fairly buzzed with a great low murmur: the Popsipetels sitting up talking of their wonderful pale-faced visitor and this strange good thing he had brought with him – *fire!*

Chapter Four
WHAT MAKES AN ISLAND FLOAT

VERY early in our experience of Popsipetel kindness we saw that if we were to get anything done at all, we would almost always have to do it secretly. The Doctor was so popular and loved by all that as soon as he showed his face at his door in the morning crowds of admirers waiting patiently outside flocked about him and followed him wherever he went. After his firemaking feat, these people expected him, I think, to be continually doing magic, and they were determined not to miss a trick.

It was only with great difficulty that we escaped from the crowd the first morning and set out with Long Arrow to explore the island at our leisure.

In the interior we found that not only the

plants and trees were suffering from the cold, the animal life was in even worst straits. Everywhere shivering birds were to be seen, their feathers all fluffed out, gathering together for flight to summer lands. And many lay dead upon the ground. Going down to the shore, we watched land crabs in large numbers taking to the sea to find some better home. While away to the south east we could see many icebergs floating – a sign that we were now not far from the terrible region of the Antarctic.

As we were looking out to sea, we noticed our friends the porpoises jumping through the waves. The Doctor hailed them and they came inshore.

He asked them how far we were from the south polar continent.

About a hundred miles, they told him. And then they asked why he wanted to know.

'Because this floating island we are on,' said he, 'is drifting southward all the time in a current. It's an island that ordinarily belongs somewhere in the tropic zone – real sultry weather, sunstrokes, and all that. If it doesn't stop going southward, pretty soon everything on it is going to perish.'

'Well,' said the porpoises, 'then the thing
to do is to get it back into a warmer climate,
isn't it?'

'Yes, but how?' said the Doctor. 'We can't
row it back.'

'No,' said they, 'but whales could push it —
if you only got enough of them.'

'What a splendid idea! Whales, the very
thing!' said the Doctor. 'Do you think you
could get me some?'

'Why, certainly,' said the porpoises. 'We
passed one herd of them out there, sporting
about among the icebergs. We'll ask them to
come over. And if they aren't enough, we'll
try and hunt up some more. Better have
plenty.'

'Thank you,' said the Doctor. 'You are very
kind. . . . By the way, do you happen to know
how this island came to be a floating island?
At least half of it, I notice, is made of stone.
It is very odd that it floats at all, isn't it?'

'It is unusual,' they said. 'But the explan-
ation is quite simple. It used to be a moun-
tainous part of South America — an overhanging part — sort of an awkward corner,
you might say. Way back in the glacial days,
thousands of years ago, it broke off from the
mainland; and by some curious accident the

inside of it, which is hollow, got filled with air as it fell into the ocean. You can see only less than half of the island: the larger part is under water. And in the middle of it, underneath, is a huge rock air chamber running right up inside the mountains. And that's what keeps it floating.'

'What a pecurious phenometer!' said Bumpo.

'It is indeed,' said the Doctor. 'I must make a note of that.' And out came the everlasting notebook.

The porpoises went bounding off towards the icebergs. And not long after, we saw the sea heaving and frothing as a big herd of whales came toward us at full speed.

They certainly were enormous creatures, and there must have been a good two hundred of them.

'Here they are,' said the porpoises, poking their head out of the water.

'Good!' said the Doctor. 'Now just explain to them, will you please, that this is a very serious matter for all the living creatures in this land. And ask them if they will be so good as to go down to the far end of the island, put their noses against it, and push it back near the coast of southern Brazil.'

The porpoises evidently succeeded in persuading the whales to do as the Doctor asked, for presently we saw them thrashing through the seas, going off towards the south end of the island.

Then we lay down upon the beach and waited.

After about an hour the Doctor got up and threw a stick into the water. For a while this floated motionless. But soon we saw it begin to move gently down the coast.

'Ah!' said the Doctor. 'See that? The island is going north at last. Thank goodness!'

Faster and faster we left the stick behind, and smaller and dimmer grew the icebergs on the skyline.

The Doctor took out his watch, threw more sticks into the water, and made a rapid calculation.

'Humph! Fourteen and a half knots an hour,' he murmured. 'A very nice speed. It should take us about five days to get back near Brazil. Well, that's that. . . . Quite a load off my mind. I declare, I feel warmer already. Let's go and get something to eat.'

Chapter Five
WAR!

ON our way back to the village the Doctor began discussing natural history with Long Arrow. But their most interesting talk, mainly about plants, had hardly begun when an Indian runner came dashing up to us with a message.

Long Arrow listened gravely to the breathless, babbled words, then turned to the Doctor and said in eagle tongue, 'Great Doctor, an evil thing has befallen the Popsipetels. Our neighbours to the south, the thievish Bag-jagderags, who for so long have cast envious eyes on our stores of ripe corn, have gone upon the warpath, and even now are advancing to attack us.'

'Evil news indeed,' said the Doctor. 'Yet let us not judge harshly. Perhaps it is that they are desperate for food, having their own crops frost-killed before harvest. For are they not even nearer the cold south than you?'

'Make no excuses for any member of the tribe of the Bag-jagderags,' said Long Arrow shaking his head. 'They are an idle, shiftless race. They do but see a chance to get corn without the labour of husbandry. If it were not that they are a much bigger tribe and hope to defeat their neighbour by sheer force of numbers, they would have not dared to make open war upon the brave Popsipetels.'

When we reached the village we found it in a great state of excitement. Everywhere men were seen putting their bows in order, sharpening spears, grinding battle-axes, and making arrows by the hundred. Women were raising a high fence of bamboo poles all round the village. Scouts and messengers kept coming and going, bringing news of the movements of the enemy. While high up in the trees and hills about the village we could see lookouts watching the mountains to the south.

Long Arrow brought another Indian, short but enormously broad, and introduced him to the Doctor as Big Teeth, the chief warrior of the Popsipetels.

The Doctor volunteered to go and see the enemy and try to argue the matter out peacefully with them instead of fighting; for war, he said, was at best a stupid, wasteful business. But the two shook their heads. Such a plan was hopeless, they said. In the last war when they had sent a messenger to do peaceful arguing, the enemy had merely hit him with an axe.

While the Doctor was asking Big Teeth how he meant to defend the village against attack, a cry of alarm was raised by the look-outs.

'They're coming! . . . The Bag-jagderags . . . swarming down the mountains in thousands!'

'Well,' said the Doctor, 'it's all in the day's work, I suppose. I don't believe in war, but if the village is attacked we must help defend it.'

And he picked up a club from the ground and tried the heft of it against a stone.

'This,' he said, 'seems like a pretty good tool to me.' And he walked to the bamboo fence and took his place among the other waiting fighters.

Then we all got hold of some kind of weapon with which to help our friends, the gallant Popsipetels: I borrowed a bow and a quiver of arrows; Jip was content to rely upon his old, but still strong teeth; Chee-Chee took a bag of rocks and climbed a palm where he could throw them down upon the enemies' heads; and Bumpo marched after the Doctor to the fence armed with a young tree in one hand and a doorpost in the other.

When the enemy drew near enough to be seen from where we stood, we all gasped with astonishment. The hillsides were actually covered with them – thousands upon thousands. They made our small army within the village look like a mere handful.

'Saints alive!' muttered Polynesia. 'Our little lot will stand no chance against that swarm. This will never do. I'm going off to get some help.'

Where she was going and what kind of help she meant to get, I had no idea. She just disappeared from my side. But Jip, who had heard her, poked his nose between the bamboo bars of the fence to get a better view of the enemy and said.

'Likely enough she's gone after the black parrots. Let's hope she finds them in time.

Just look at those ugly ruffians climbing down the rocks – millions of 'em! This fight's going to keep us all hopping.'

And Jip was right. Before a quarter of an hour had gone by, our village was completely surrounded by one huge mob of yelling, raging Bag-jagderags.

I now come again to a part in the story of our voyages where things happened so quickly, one upon the other, that looking backwards I see the picture only in a confused kind of way. I know that if it had not been for the Terrible Three – as they came afterwards to be fondly called in Popsipetel history – Long Arrow, Bumpo, and the Doctor, the war would have been soon over and the whole island would have belonged to the worthless Bag-jagderags. But the Englishman, the African, and the Indian were a regiment in themselves, and between them they made that village a dangerous place for any man to try to enter.

The bamboo fencing that had been hastily set up round the town was not a very strong affair, and right from the start it gave way in one place after another as the enemy thronged and crowded against it. Then the Doctor, Long Arrow, and Bumpo would

'The Terrible Three'

From an Indian rock engraving found on Hawk's-Head Mountain, Spider Monkey Island

hurry to the weak spot, a terrific hand-to-hand fight would take place, and the enemy be thrown out. But almost instantly a cry of alarm would come from some other part of the village wall; and the Three would have to rush off and do the same thing all over again.

The Popsipetels were themselves no mean fighters, but the strength and weight of those three men of different lands, standing close together, swinging their enormous war clubs, was really a sight for the wonder and admiration of anyone.

Many weeks later when I was passing an Indian campfire at night I heard this song being sung. It has since become one of the traditional folksongs of the Popsipetels.

The Song of the Terrible Three

Oh, hear ye the song of the Terrible Three
And the fight they fought by the edge of the sea.
Down from the mountains, the rocks and the crags,
Swarming like wasps, came the Bag-jagderags.

Surrounding our village, our walls they broke down.
Oh, sad was the plight of our men and our town!
But Heaven determined our land to set free
And sent us the help of the Terrible Three.

Shoulder to shoulder, they hammered and hit.
Like demons of fury they kicked and they bit.
Like a wall of destruction they stood in a row,
Flattening enemies, six at a blow.

And long shall we sing of the Terrible Three
And the fight that they fought by the edge of the sea.

Chapter Six
GENERAL POLYNESIA

BUT, alas, even the Three, mighty though they were, could not last forever against an army that seemed to have no end. In one of the hottest scrimmages, when the enemy had broken a particularly wide hole through the fence, I saw Long Arrow's great figure topple and come down with a spear sticking in his broad chest.

For another half hour Bumpo and the Doctor fought on side by side. How their strength held out so long I cannot tell, for never a second were they given to get their breath or rest their arms.

The Doctor – the quiet, kindly, peaceable little Doctor! – Well, you wouldn't have known him if you had seen him that day dealing out whacks you could hear a mile off, walloping and swatting in all directions.

As for Bumpo, with staring eyeballs and grim set teeth, he was a veritable demon. None dared come within yards of that wicked, wide-circling doorpost. But a stone, skilfully thrown, struck him at last in the centre of the forehead. And down went the second of the Three. John Dolittle, the last of the Terribles, was left fighting alone.

Jip and I rushed to his side and tried to take the places of the fallen ones. But far too light and too small, we made but a poor exchange. Another length of the fence crashed down, and through the widened gap the Bag-jagderags poured in on us like a flood.

'To the canoes! To the sea!' shouted the Popsipetels. 'Fly for your lives! All is over! The war is lost!'

But the Doctor and I never got a chance to fly for our lives. We were swept off our feet and knocked down flat by the sheer weight of the mob. And once down, we were unable to get up again. I thought we would surely be trampled to death.

But at that moment, above the din and racket of the battle, we heard the most terrifying noise that ever assaulted human ears: the sound of millions and millions of parrots all screeching with fury together.

The army, which in the nick of time Polynesia had brought to our rescue, darkened the whole sky to the west. I asked her afterwards how many birds there were, and she said she didn't know exactly but they certainly numbered somewhere between sixty and seventy million. In that extraordinarly short space of time she had brought them from the mainland of South America.

If you have ever heard a parrot screech with anger, you will know that it makes a truly frightful sound; and if you have ever been bitten by one, you will know that its bite can be a nasty and a painful thing.

The black parrots (coal-black all over, they were — except for a scarlet beak and a streak of red in wing and tail) on the word of command from Polynesia set to work upon the Bag-jagderags who were now pouring through the village looking for plunder.

And the black parrots' method of fighting was peculiar. This is what they did: on the head of each Bag-jagderag three or four parrots settled and took a good foothold in his hair with their claws; then they leaned down over the sides of his head and began clipping snips out of his ears, for all the world as though they were punching tickets. That is all they did. They never bit them anywhere else except the ears. But it won the war for us.

With howls pitiful to hear, the Bag-jagderags fell over one another in their haste to get out of that accursed village. It was no use their trying to pull the parrots off their heads because for each head there were always four more parrots waiting impatiently to get on.

Some of the enemy were lucky, and with only a snip or two managed to get outside the fence – where the parrots immediately left them alone. But with most, before the black birds had done with them, the ears presented a very singular appearance – like the edge of a postage stamp. This treatment, very painful at the time, did not however do them any permanent harm beyond the change in looks. And it later got to be the tribal mark of the Bag-jagderags. No really smart young lady of this tribe would be seen walking with a man who did not have scalloped ears – for such was a proof that he had been in the Great War. And that (though it is not generally known to scientists) is how this people came be called by the other Indian nations, the *Ragged-Eared Bag-jagderags*.

As soon as the village was cleared of the enemy the Doctor turned his attention to the wounded.

In spite of the length and fierceness of the struggle, there were surprisingly few serious injuries. Poor Long Arrow was the worst off. However, after the Doctor had washed his wound and got him to bed, he opened his eyes and said he already felt better. Bumpo was only badly stunned.

With this part of the business over, the Doctor called to Polynesia to have the black parrots drive the enemy right back into their own country and to wait there, guarding them all night.

Polynesia gave the short word of command, and like one bird those millions of parrots opened their red beaks and let out once more their terrifying battle scream.

The Bag-jagderags didn't wait to be bitten a second time, but fled helter-skelter over the mountains from which they had come, whilst Polynesia and her victorious army followed watchfully behind like a great threatening black cloud.

The Doctor picked up his high hat which had been knocked off in the fight, dusted it carefully, and put it on.

'Tomorrow,' he said, shaking his fist towards the hills, 'we will arrange the terms of peace – and we will arrange them – in the City of Bag-jagderag!'

His words were greeted with cheers of triumph from the admiring Popsipetels. The war was over.

Chapter Seven
THE PEACE OF THE PARROTS

THE next day we set out for the far end of the island, and reaching it in canoes (for we went by sea) after a journey of twenty-five hours, we remained no longer than was necessary in the City of Bag-jagderag.

When he threw himself into that fight at Popsipetel, I saw the Doctor really angry for the first time in my life. But his anger, once aroused, was slow to die. All the way down the coast of the island he never ceased to rail against this cowardly people who had attacked his friends, the Popsipetels, for no other reason but to rob them of their corn because they were too idle to till the land themselves. And he was still angry when he reached the City of Bag-jagderag.

Long Arrow had not come with us, for he was as yet too weak from his wound. But the Doctor — always clever at languages — was already getting familiar with the Indian tongue. Besides, among the half-dozen Popsipetels who accompanied us to paddle the canoes, was one boy to whom he had taught a little English. He and the Doctor between them managed to make themselves understood to the Bag-jagderags. These people — with the terrible parrots still blackening the hills about their stone town, waiting for the word to descend and attack — were, we found, in a very humble mood.

Leaving our canoes we passed up the main street to the palace of the chief. Bumpo and I couldn't help smiling with satisfaction as we saw how the waiting crowds that lined the roadway bowed their heads to the ground as the little, round, angry figure of the Doctor strutted ahead of us with his chin in the air.

At the foot of the palace steps the chief and all the more important personages of the tribe were waiting to meet him, smiling humbly and holding out their hands in friendliness. The Doctor took not the slightest notice. He marched right by them, up the steps to the door of the palace. There he turned round and at once began to address the people in a firm voice.

I never heard such a speech in my life — and I am quite sure that they never did, either. First he called them a long string of names: cowards, loafers, thieves, vagabonds, good-for-nothings, bullies, and whatnot. Then he said he was still seriously thinking of allowing the parrots to drive them on into the sea in order that this pleasant land might be rid, once for all, of their worthless carcasses.

At this a great cry for mercy went up, and the chief and all of them fell on their knees, calling out that they would submit to any conditions of peace he wished.

Then the Doctor called for one of their scribes — that is, a man who did picture-writing. And on the stone walls of the palace of Bag-jagderag he bade him write down the terms of the peace as he dictated it. This peace is known as *The Peace of the Parrots*, and — unlike most peaces — was, and is, strictly kept — even to this day.

It was quite long in words. The half of the palace front was covered with picture-writing, and fifty pots of paint were used before the weary scribe had done. But the main part of it all was that there should be no more fighting and that the two tribes should give solemn promise to help one another whenever there was corn famine or other distress in the lands belonging to either.

This greatly surprised the Bag-jagderags. They had expected from the Doctor's angry face that he would at least chop a couple of hundred heads off – and probably make the rest of them slaves for life.

But when they saw that he only meant kindly by them, their great fear of him changed to a tremendous admiration. And as he ended his long speech and walked briskly down the steps again on his way back to the canoes, the group of chieftains threw themselves at his feet and cried, 'Do but stay with us, Great Lord, and all the riches of Bag-jagderag shall be poured into your lap. Gold mines we know of in the mountains and pearl beds beneath the sea. Only stay with us, that your all-powerful wisdom may lead our Council and our people in prosperity and peace.'

The Doctor held up his hand for silence.

'No man,' said he, 'would wish to be the

guest of the Bag-jagderags till they had proved by their deeds that they are an honest race. Be true to the terms of the Peace and from yourselves shall come good government and prosperity. Farewell!'

Then he turned and followed by Bumpo, the Popsipetels, and myself, walked rapidly down to the canoes.

Chapter Eight
THE HANGING STONE

BUT the change of heart in the Bag-jagderags was really sincere. The Doctor had made a great impression on them — a deeper one than even he himself realized at the time. In fact, I sometimes think that that speech of his from the palace steps had more effect upon the Indians of Spider Monkey Island than had any of his great deed which, great though they were, were always magnified and exaggerated when the news of them was passed from mouth to mouth.

A sick girl was brought to him as he reached the place where the boats lay. She turned out to have some quite simple ailment which he quickly gave the remedy for. But this increased his popularity still.

more. And when he stepped into his canoe, the people all around us actually burst into tears. It seems (I learned this afterwards) that they thought he was going away across the sea for good, to the mysterious foreign lands from which he had come.

Some of the chieftains spoke to the Popsipetels as we pushed off. What they said I did not understand, but we noticed that several canoes filled with Bag-jagderags followed us at a respectful distance all the way back to Popsipetel.

The Doctor had determined to return by the other shore, so that we should be thus able to make a complete trip round the island's shores.

Shortly after we started, while still off the lower end of the island, we sighted a steep point on the coast where the sea was in a great state of turmoil, white with soapy froth. On going nearer, we found that this was caused by our friendly whales who were still faithfully working away with their noses against the end of the island, driving us northward. We had been kept so busy with the war that we had forgotten all about them. But as we paused and watched their mighty tails lashing and churning the sea,

'Working away with their noses against the end
of the island'

we suddenly realized that we had not felt cold in quite a long while. Speeding up our boat lest the island be carried away from us altogether, we passed on up the coast; and here and there we noticed that the trees on the shore already looked greener and more healthy. Spider Monkey Island was getting back in to her home climates.

About halfway to Popsipetel we went ashore and spent two or three days exploring the central part of the island. Our Indian paddlers took us up into the mountains, very steep and high in this region, overhanging the sea. And they showed us what they called the Whispering Rocks.

This was a very peculiar and striking piece of scenery. It was like a great vast basin, in the mountains, and out of the centre of it there rose a table of rock with an ivory chair upon it. All around this the mountain went up like stairs, or theatre seats, to a great height – except at one narrow end, which was open to a view of the sea. You could imagine it a council place or concert hall for giants, and the rock table in the centre the stage for performers or the stand for the speaker.

We asked our guides why it was called the

'The Whispering Rocks'

Whispering Rocks, and they said, 'Go down into it and we will show you.'

The great bowl was miles deep and miles wide. We scrambled down the rocks and they showed us how, even when you stood far, far apart from one another, you merely had to whisper in that great place and everyone in the theatre could hear you. This was, the Doctor said, on account of the echoes which played backwards and forwards between the high walls of rock.

Our guides told us that it was here, in days long gone by when the Popsipetels owned the whole of Spider Monkey Island, that the kings were crowned. The ivory chair upon the table was the throne on which they sat. And so great was the big theatre that all the Indians in the island were able to get seats in it to see the ceremony.

They showed us also an enormous hanging stone perched on the edge of a volcano's crater – the highest summit in the whole island. Although it was very far below us, we could see it quite plainly, and it looked wobbly enough to be pushed off its perch with the hand. There was a legend among the people, they said, that when the greatest of all Popsipetel kings should be crowned in the ivory chair, this hanging stone would tumble into the volcano's mouth and go straight down to the centre of the earth.

The Doctor said he would like to go and examine it closer.

And when we had come to the lip of the volcano (it took us half a day to get up to it), we found the stone was unbelievably large — big as a cathedral. Underneath it we could look right down into a black hole that seemed to have no bottom. The Doctor explained to us that volcanoes sometimes spurted up fire from these holes in their tops, but that those on floating islands were always cold and dead.

'Stubbins,' he said, looking up at the great stone towering above us, 'do you know what would most likely happen if that boulder should fall in?'

'No,' said I, 'what?'

'You remember the air chamber which the porpoises told us lies under the centre of the island?'

'Yes.'

'Well, this stone is heavy enough, if it fell into the volcano, to break through into that air chamber from above. And once it did, the air would escape and the floating island would float no more. It would sink.'

'But then everybody on it would be drowned, wouldn't they?' said Bumpo.

'Oh, no, not necessarily. That would depend on the depth of the sea where the sinking took place. The island might touch the bottom when it had only gone down, say a hundred feet. But there would be lots of it still sticking up above the water then, wouldn't there?'

'Yes,' said Bumpo. 'I suppose there would. Well, let us hope that the ponderous fragment does *not* lose its equilibriosity, for I don't believe it would stop at the centre of the earth. More likely, it would fall right through the world and come out the other side.'

Many other wonders there were that these people showed us in the central regions of their island. But I have not time or space to tell you of them now.

Descending towards the shore again, we noticed that we were still being watched, even here among the highlands, by the Bagjagderags who had followed us. And when we put to sea once more a boatload of them proceeded to go ahead of us in the direction of Popsipetel. Having lighter canoes, they travelled faster than our party, and we judged that they should reach the village — if that was where they were going — many hours before we could.

The Doctor was now becoming anxious to see how Long Arrow was getting on, so we all took turns at the paddles and went on travelling by moonlight through the whole night.

We reached Popsipetel just as the dawn was breaking.

To our great surprise we found that not only we, but the whole village also, had been up all night. A great crowd was gathered about the dead chief's house. And as we landed our canoes upon the beach we saw a large number of old men, the seniors of the tribe, coming out at the main door.

We inquired what was the meaning of all this and were told that the election of a new chief had been going on all through the whole night. Bumpo asked the name of the new chief, but this, it seemed, had not yet been given out. It would be announced at midday.

As soon as the Doctor had paid a visit to Long Arrow and seen that he was doing nicely, we proceeded to our own house at the far end of the village. Here we ate some breakfast and then lay down to take a good rest.

Rest, indeed, we needed, for life had been strenuous and busy for us ever since we had landed on the island. And it wasn't many minutes after our weary heads struck the pillows that the whole crew of us were sound asleep.

Chapter Nine
THE ELECTION

WE were awakened by music. The glaring noonday sunlight was streaming in at our door, outside which some kind of band appeared to be playing.

We got up and looked out. Our house was surrounded by the whole population of Popsipetel. We were used to having quite a number of curious and admiring Indians waiting at our door at all hours, but this was quite different. The vast crowd was dressed in its best clothes. Bright beads, gaudy feathers, and gay blankets gave cheerful colour to the scene. Everyone seemed in very good humour, singing or playing on musical instruments – mostly painted wooden whistles or drums made from skins.

We found Polynesia – who while we slept

had arrived back from Bag-jagderag – sitting on our doorpost watching the show. We asked her what all the holiday-making was about.

'The result of the election has just been announced,' said she. 'The name of the new chief was given out at noon.'

'And who is the new chief?' asked the Doctor.'

'You are,' said Polynesia quietly.

'I!' gasped the Doctor – 'Well, of all things!'

'Yes,' said she. 'You're the one. – And what's more, they've changed your surname for you. They didn't think that Dolittle was a proper or respectful name for a man who had done so much. So you are now to be known as Jong Thinkalot. How do you like it?'

'But I don't *want* to be a chief,' said the Doctor in an irritable voice.

'I'm afraid you'll have hard work to get out of it now,' said she – 'unless you're willing to put to sea again in one of their rickety canoes. You see you've been elected not merely the Chief of the Popsipetels, you're to be a king – the King of the whole of Spider Monkey Island. The Bag-jagderags, who were so anxious to have you govern them, sent spies and messengers ahead of

you; and when they found that you had been
elected Chief of the Popsipetels overnight
they were bitterly disappointed. However,
rather than lose you altogether, the Bag-
jagderags were willing to give up their
independence and insisted that they and
their lands be united to the Popsipetels in
order that you could be made king of both.
So now you're in for it.'

'Oh, Lord!' groaned the Doctor. 'I do wish
they wouldn't be so enthusiastic! Bother it,
I don't *want* to be a king!'

'I should think, Doctor,' said I, 'you'd feel
rather proud and glad. I wish *I* had a chance
to be a king.'

'Oh, I know it sounds grand,' said he, pull-
ing on his boots miserably. 'But the trouble
is, you can't take up responsibilities and
then just drop them again when you feel like
it. I have my own work to do. Scarcely one
moment have I had to give to natural history
since I landed on this island. I've been doing
someone else's business all the time. And
now they want me to go on doing it! Why,
once I'm made King of the Popsipetels, that's
the end of me as a useful naturalist. I'd be
too busy for anything. All I'd be then is just
a . . . er . . . er . . . just a king.'

'Well, that's something!' said Bumpo. 'My father is a king and has a hundred and twenty wives.'

'That would make it worse,' said the Doctor — 'a hundred and twenty times worse. I have my work to do. I don't want to be a king.'

'Look,' said Polynesia, 'here come the head men to announce your election. Hurry up and get your boots laced.'

The throng before our door had suddenly parted asunder, making a long lane, and down this we now saw a group of personages coming toward us. The man in front, a handsome old Indian with a wrinkled face, carried in his hands a wooden crown — a truly beautiful and gorgeous crown, even though of wood. Wonderfully carved and painted, it had two lovely blue feathers springing from the front of it. Behind the old man came eight strong Indians bearing a litter, a sort of chair with long handles underneath to carry it by.

Kneeling down on one knee, bending his head almost to the ground, the old man addressed the Doctor, who now stood in the doorway putting on his collar and tie.

'Oh Mighty One,' said he, 'we bring you word from the Popsipetel people. Great are

your deeds beyond belief, kind is your heart
and your wisdom, deeper than the sea. Our
chief is dead. The people clamour for a
worthy leader. Our old enemies, the Bag-
jagderags are become, through you, our
brothers and good friends. They too desire to
bask beneath the sunshine of your smile.
Behold then, I bring you the Sacred Crown
of Popsipetel that, since ancient days when
this island and its peoples were one,
beneath one monarch, has rested on no
kingly brow. Oh Kindly One, we are bidden
by the united voices of the peoples of this
land to carry you to the Whispering Rocks,
that there, with all respect and majesty, you
may be crowned our king – King of all the
Moving Land.'

The good Indians did not seem to have
even considered the possibility of John
Dolittle's refusing. As for the poor Doctor, I
never saw him so upset by anything. It was
in fact the only time I have known him to
get thoroughly fussed.

'Oh, dear!' I heard him murmur, looking
around wildly for some escape. 'What *shall*
I do? . . . Did any of you see where I laid that
stud of mine? . . . How on earth can I get this
collar on without a stud? What a day this is,

to be sure! . . . Maybe it rolled under the bed, Bumpo. . . . I do think they might have given me a day or so to think it over in. Whoever heard of waking a man right out of his sleep and telling him he's got to be a king, before he has even washed his face? . . . Can't any of you find it? Maybe you're standing on it, Bumpo. Move your feet.'

'Oh don't bother about your stud,' said Polynesia. 'You will have to be crowned without a collar. They won't know the difference.'

'I tell you I'm not going to be crowned,' cried the Doctor —'not if I can help it. I'll make them a speech. Perhaps that will satisfy them.'

He turned back to the Indians at the door.

'My friends,' he said, 'I am not worthy of this great honour you would do me. Little or no skill have I in the arts of kingcraft. Assuredly among your own brave men you will find many better fitted to lead you. For this compliment, this confidence and trust, I thank you. But, I pray you, do not think of me for such high duties which I could not possibly fulfil.'

The old man repeated his words to the people behind him in a louder voice. Stolidly

they shook their heads, moving not an inch.
The old man turned back to the Doctor.

'You are the chosen one,' he said. 'They
will have none but you.'

Into the Doctor's perplexed face suddenly
there came a flash of hope.

'I'll go and see Long Arrow,' he whispered
to me. 'Perhaps he will know of some way to
get me out of this.'

And asking the personages to excuse him
a moment, he left them there, standing at
his door, and hurried off in the direction of
Long Arrow's house. I followed him.

We found our big friend lying on a grass
bed outside his home, where he had been
moved so that he might witness the holiday-
making.

'Long Arrow,' said the Doctor speaking
quickly in eagle tongue so that the bystanders
should not overhear, 'in dire peril I come to
you for help. These men would make me
their king. If such a thing befall me, all the
great work I hoped to do must go undone, for
who is there unfreer than a king? I pray you
speak with them and persuade their kind
well-meaning hearts that what they plan to
do would be unwise.'

Long Arrow raised himself upon his elbow.

'Oh Kindly One,' said he (this seemed now to have become the usual manner of address when speaking to the Doctor), 'sorely it grieves me that the first wish you ask of me I should be unable to grant. Alas! I can do nothing. These people have so set their hearts on keeping you for king that if I tried to interfere they would drive me from their land and likely crown you in the end in any case. A king you must be, if only for a while. We must so arrange the business of governing that you may have time to give to nature's secrets. Later we may be able to hit upon some plan to relieve you of the burden of the crown. But for now you must be king. These people are a headstrong tribe and they will have their way. There is no other course.'

Sadly the Doctor turned away from the bed and faced about. And there behind him stood the old man again, the crown still held in his wrinkled hands and the royal litter waiting at his elbow. With a deep reverence the bearers motioned towards the seat of the chair, inviting the Doctor to get in.

Once more the poor Doctor looked wildly, hopelessly about him for some means of escape. For a moment I thought he was going to take to his heels and run for it. But the crowd around us was far too thick and densely packed for anyone to break through it. A band of whistles and drums nearby suddenly started the music of a solemn processional march. He turned back pleadingly again to Long Arrow in a last appeal for help. But the big Indian merely shook his head and pointed, like the bearers, to the waiting chair.

At last, almost in tears, John Dolittle stepped slowly into the litter and sat down. As he was hoisted on to the broad shoulders of the bearers I heard him still feebly muttering beneath his breath, 'Botheration take it! I don't *want* to be a king!'

'Farewell!' called Long Arrow from his bed. 'And may good fortune ever stand within the shadow of your throne!'

'He comes! He comes!' murmured the crowd. 'Away! Away! To the Whispering Rocks!'

And as the procession formed up to leave the village, the crowd about us began hurrying off in the direction of the mountains to make sure of good seats in the giant theatre where the crowning ceremony would take place.

Chapter Ten
THE CORONATION OF KING JONG

IN my long lifetime I have seen many grand and inspiring things, but never anything that impressed me half as much as the sight of the Whispering Rocks as they looked on the day King Jong was crowned. As Bumpo, Chee-Chee, Polynesia, Jip and I finally reached the dizzy edge of the great bowl and looked down inside it, it was like gazing over a never-ending ocean of copper-coloured faces, for every seat in the theatre was filled; every man, woman and child in the island — including Long Arrow who had been carried up on his sickbed — was there to see the show.

Yet not a sound, not a pin-drop, disturbed the solemn silence of the Whispering Rocks. It was quite creepy and sent chills running up and down your spine. Bumpo told me afterwards that it took his breath away too much for him to speak, but that he hadn't known before that there were that many people in the world.

Away down by the Table of the Throne stood a brand-new, brightly coloured totem pole. All the Indian families had totem poles and kept them set up before the doors of their houses. The idea of a totem pole is something like a doorplate or a visiting card. It represents in its carvings the deeds and qualities of the family to which it belongs. This one, beautifully decorated and much higher than any other, was the Dolittle or, as it was to be henceforth called, the Royal Thinkalot totem. It had nothing but animals on it, to signify the Doctor's great knowledge of creatures. And the animals chosen to represent good qualities of character, such as the deer for speed; the ox for perseverance; the fish for discretion, and so on. But at the top of the totem is always placed the sign or animal by which the family is most proud to be known. This, on the Thinkalot pole, was an enormous parrot, in memory of the famous Peace of the Parrots.

The Ivory Throne had been all polished

with scented oil and it glistened whitely in the strong sunlight. At the foot of it there had been strewn great quantities of branches of flowering trees, which with the new warmth of milder climates were now blossoming in the valleys of the island.

Soon we saw the royal litter, with the Doctor seated in it, slowly ascending the winding steps of the Table. Reaching the flat top at last, it halted and the Doctor stepped out upon the flowery carpet. So still and perfect was the silence that even at that distance above I distinctly heard a twig snap beneath his tread.

Walking to the throne accompanied by the old man, the Doctor got up upon the stand and sat down. How tiny his little round figure looked when seen from that tremendous height! The throne had been made for longer-legged kings, and when he was seated, his feet did not reach the ground but dangled six inches from the top step.

Then the old man turned round and looking up at the people began to speak in a quiet, even voice, but every word he said was easily heard in the farthest corner of the Whispering Rocks.

First he recited the names of all the great

Popsipetel kings who in days long ago had been crowned in this ivory chair. He spoke of the greatness of the Popsipetel people, of their triumphs, of their hardships. Then waving his hand towards the Doctor he began recounting the things which this king-to-be had done. And I am bound to say that they easily outmatched the deeds of those who had gone before him.

As soon as he started to speak of what the Doctor had achieved for the tribe, the people, still strictly silent, all began waving their right hands towards the throne. This gave to the vast theatre a very singular appearance: acres and acres of something moving – with never a sound.

At last the old man finished his speech and stepping up to the chair, very respectfully removed the Doctor's battered high hat. He was about to put it upon the ground, but the Doctor took it from him hastily and kept it on his lap. Then taking up the Sacred Crown he placed it upon John Dolittle's head. It did not fit very well (for it had been made for smaller-headed kings), and when the wind blew in freshly from the sunlit sea the Doctor had some difficulty in keeping it on. But it looked very splendid.

Turning once more to the people, the old man said,

'People of Popsipetel, behold your elected king! . . . Are you content?'

And then at last the voice of the people broke loose.

'JONG! JONG!' they shouted. 'LONG LIVE KING JONG!'

The sound burst upon the solemn silence with the crash of a hundred cannons. There, where even a whisper carried miles, the shock of it was like a blow in the face. Back and forth the mountains threw it to one another. I thought the echoes of it would never die away as it passed rumbling through the whole island, jangling among the lower valleys, booming in the distant sea caves.

Suddenly I saw the old man point upward, to the highest mountain in the island; and looking over my shoulder, I was just in time to see the Hanging Stone topple slowly out of sight – down into the heart of the volcano.

'See ye, People of the Moving Land!' the old man cried. 'The stone has fallen and our legend has come true: the King of Kings is crowned this day!'

The Doctor too had seen the stone fall and he was now standing up looking at the sea expectantly.

'He's thinking of the air chamber,' said Bumpo in my ear. 'Let us hope that the sea isn't very deep in these parts.'

After a full minute (so long did it take the stone to fall that depth) we heard a muffled, distant, crunching thud – and then, immediately after, a great hissing of escaping air. The Doctor, his face tense with anxiety, sat down on the throne again still watching the blue water of the ocean with staring eyes.

Soon we felt the island slowly sinking beneath us. We saw the sea creep inland over the beaches as the shores went down – one foot, three feet, ten feet, twenty, fifty, a hundred. And then, thank goodness, gently as a butterfly alighting on a rose, it stopped! Spider Monkey Island had come to rest on the sandy bottom of the Atlantic, and earth was joined to earth once more.

Of course many of the houses near the shores were now under water. Popsipetel Village itself had entirely disappeared. But it didn't matter. No one was drowned, for every soul in the island was high up in the hills watching the coronation of King Jong.

The Indians themselves did not realize at the time what was taking place, though of course they had felt the land sinking beneath them. The Doctor told us afterwards that it must have been the shock of that tremendous shout, coming from a million throats at once, which had toppled the Hanging Stone off its perch. But in Popsipetel history the story was handed down (and it is firmly believed to this day) that when King Jong sat upon the throne, so great was his mighty weight that the very island itself sank down to do him honour and never moved again.

PART VI

Chapter One
NEW POPSIPETEL

JONG THINKALOT had not ruled over his new kingdom for more than a couple of days before my notions about kings and the kinds of lives they led changed very considerably. I had thought that all that kings had to do was to sit on a throne and have people bow down before them several times a day. I now saw that a king can be the hardest-working man in the world — if he attends properly to his business.

From the moment that he got up early in the morning till the time he went to bed late at night — seven days in the week — John Dolittle was busy, busy, busy. First of all, there was the new town to be built. The village of Popsipetel had disappeared: the City of New Popsipetel must be made. With great care a place was chosen for it – and a very beautiful position it was, at the mouth of a large river. The shores of the island at this point formed a lovely wide bay where canoes – and ships, too, if they should ever come – could lie peacefully at anchor without danger from storms.

In building this town the Doctor gave the Indians a lot of new ideas. He showed them what town sewers were and how garbage should be collected each day and burned. High up in the hills he made a large lake by damming a stream. This was the water supply for the town. None of these things had the Indians ever seen, and many of the sicknesses that they had suffered from before were now entirely prevented by proper drainage and pure drinking water.

Peoples who don't use fire, do not, of course, have metals either because without fire it is almost impossible to shape iron and steel. One of the first things that John Dolittle did was to search the mountains till he found iron and copper mines. Then he set to work to teach the Indians how these metals could be melted and made into knives and ploughs and water pipes and all manner of things.

In his kingdom the Doctor tried his hardest to do away with most of the old-fashioned pomp and grandeur of a royal court. As he said to Bumpo and me, if he must be a king he meant to be a thoroughly democratic one, that is, a king who is chummy and friendly with his subjects and doesn't put on airs. And when he drew up the plans for the City of New Popsipetel he had no palace shown of any kind. A little cottage in a back street was all that he had provided for himself.

But this the Indians would not permit on any account. They had been used to having their kings rule in a truly grand and kingly manner, and they insisted that he have built for himself the most magnificent palace ever seen. In all else they let him have his own way absolutely, but they wouldn't allow him to wriggle out of any ceremony or show that goes with being a king. A thousand servants he had to keep in his palace, night and day, to wait on him. The Royal Canoe had to be kept up – a gorgeous, polished mahogany boat, seventy feet long, inlaid with mother-of-pearl and paddled by the hundred strongest men in the island. The palace gardens covered a square mile and employed a hundred and sixty gardeners.

Even in his dress the poor man was compelled always to be grand and elegant and uncomfortable. The beloved and battered high hat was put away in a closet and looked at secretly. State robes had to be worn on all occasions. And when the Doctor did once in a while manage to sneak off for a short natural-history expedition he never dared to wear his old clothes, but had to chase his butterflies with a crown upon his head and a scarlet cloak flying behind him in the wind.

There was no end to the kinds of duties the Doctor had to perform and the questions he had to decide upon – everything from settling disputes about lands and boundaries to making peace between husband and wife who had been throwing shoes at one another. In the east wing of the Royal Palace was the Hall of Justice. And here King Jong sat every morning from nine to eleven passing judgment on all cases that were brought before him.

Then in the afternoon he taught school. The sort of things he taught were not always those you find in ordinary schools. Grown-ups as well as children came to learn.

'Had to chase his butterflies with a crown upon his head'

Bumpo and I helped with the teaching as far as we could – simple arithmetic and easy things like that. But the classes in astronomy, farming science, the proper care of babies, with a host of other subjects, the Doctor had to teach himself. The Indians were tremendously keen about the schooling and they came in droves and crowds, so that even with the open-air classes (a schoolhouse was impossible of course) the Doctor had to take them in relays and batches of five or six thousand at a time and used a big megaphone or trumpet to make himself heard.

The rest of his day was more than filled with road making, building water mills, attending the sick, and a million other things.

In spite of his being so unwilling to become a king, John Dolittle made a very good one – once he got started. He may not have been as dignified as many kings in history who were always running off to war and getting themselves into romantic situations, but since I have grown up and seen something of foreign lands and governments I have often thought that Popsipetel under the reign of Jong Thinkalot was perhaps the best-ruled state in the history of the world.

The Doctor's birthday came round after we had been on the island six months and a half. The people made a great public holiday of it and there was much feasting, dancing, fireworks, speech-making, and jollification.

Towards the close of the day the chief men of the two tribes formed a procession and passed through the streets of the town, carrying a very gorgeously painted tablet of ebony wood, ten feet high. This was a picture history, such as they preserved for each of the ancient kings of Popsipetel to record their deeds.

With great and solemn ceremony it was set up over the door of the new palace and everybody then clustered around to look at it. It had six pictures on it commemorating the six great events in the life of King Jong and beneath were written the verses that explained them. They were composed by the Court Poet, and this is a translation:

I

His Landing on the Island

Heaven-sent,
In his dolphin-drawn canoe

From worlds unknown
He landed on our shores.
The very palms
Bowed down their heads
In welcome to the coming King.

II
His Meeting with the Beetle

By moonlight in the mountains
He communed with beasts.
The shy jabizri brings him picture-words
Of great distress.

III
He Liberates the Lost Families

Big was his heart with pity;
Big were his hands with strength.
See how he tears the mountain like a yam!
See how the lost ones
Dance forth to greet the day!

IV
He Makes Fire

Our land was cold and dying.
He waved his hand, and lo!
Lightning leapt from the cloudless skies;
The sun leaned down;
And fire was born!

Then while we crowded round
The grateful glow, pushed he
Our wayward, floating land
Back to peaceful anchorage
In sunny seas.

V

He Leads the People to Victory in War
Once only
Was his kindly countenance
Darkened by a deadly frown.
Woe to the wicked enemy
That dares attack
The tribe with Thinkalot for Chief!

VI

He Is Crowned King
The birds of the air rejoiced;
The sea laughed and gambolled with her
    shores;
All people wept for joy
The day we crowned him King.
He is the Builder, the Healer, the Teacher,
    and the Prince;
He is the greatest of them all.
May he live a thousand thousand years,
Happy in his heart,
To bless our land with peace.

Chapter Two
THOUGHTS OF HOME

IN the Royal Palace Bumpo and I had a beautiful suite of rooms of our very own — which Polynesia, Jip, and Chee-Chee shared with us. Officially, Bumpo was Minister of the Interior, while I was First Lord of the Treasury. Long Arrow also had quarters there, but at present he was absent, travelling abroad.

One night after supper when the Doctor was away in the town somewhere visiting a newborn baby, we were all sitting round the big table in Bumpo's reception room. This we did every evening, to talk over the plans for the following day and various affairs of state. It was a kind of cabinet meeting.

Tonight however we were talking about England — and also about things to eat. We had got a little tired of Indian food. You see, none of the natives knew how to cook, and we had the most discouraging time training a chef for the Royal Kitchen. Most of them were champions at spoiling good food. Often we got so hungry that the Doctor would sneak downstairs with us into the palace basement, after all the cooks were safe in bed, and fry pancakes secretly over the dying embers of the fire. The Doctor himself was the finest cook that ever lived. But he used to make a terrible mess of the kitchen, and of course we had to be awfully careful that we didn't get caught.

Well, as I was saying, tonight food was the subject of discussion at the cabinet meeting, and I had just been reminding Bumpo of the nice dishes we had had at the bed maker's house in Monteverde.

'I tell you what I would like now,' said Bumpo, 'a large cup of cocoa with whipped cream on the top of it. In Oxford we used to be able to get the most wonderful cocoa. It is really too bad they haven't any cocoa trees in this island, or cows to give cream.'

'When do you suppose,' asked Jip, 'the Doctor intends to move on from here?'

'I was talking to him about that only

yesterday,' said Polynesia. 'But I couldn't get any satisfactory answer out of him. He didn't seem to want to speak about it.'

There was a pause in the conversation.

'Do you know what I believe?' she added presently. 'I believe the Doctor has given up even thinking of going home.'

'Good Lord!' cried Bumpo. 'You don't say!'

'Sh!' said Polynesia. 'What's that noise?'

We listened, and away off in the distant corridors of the palace we heard the sentries crying, 'The King! Make way! The King!'

'It's he – at last,' whispered Polynesia. 'Late, as usual. Poor man, how he does work! Chee-Chee, get the pipe and tobacco out of the cupboard and lay the dressing gown ready on his chair.'

When the Doctor came into the room he looked serious and thoughtful. Wearily he took off his crown and hung it on a peg behind the door. Then he exchanged the royal cloak for the dressing gown, dropped into his chair at the head of the table with a deep sigh, and started to fill his pipe.

'Well,' asked Polynesia quietly, 'how did you find the baby?'

'The baby?' he murmured – his thoughts still seemed to be very far away. 'Ah, yes.

The baby was much better, thank you. It has
cut its second tooth.'

Then he was silent again, staring dreamily
at the ceiling through a cloud of tobacco
smoke, while we all sat round quite still,
waiting.

'We were wondering, Doctor,' I said at
last – 'just before you came in – when
you would be starting home again. We will
have been on this island seven months
tomorrow.'

The Doctor sat forward in his chair looking rather uncomfortable.

'Well, as a matter of fact,' said he after a
moment, 'I meant to speak to you myself
this evening on that very subject. But it's –
er – a little hard to make anyone exactly
understand the situation. I am afraid that it
would be impossible for me to leave the
work I am now engaged on. . . . You
remember when they first insisted on
making me king, I told you it was not easy
to shake off responsibilities once you had
taken them up. These people have come to
rely on me for a great number of things. We
have, one might say, changed the current of
their lives considerably. Now it is a very
ticklish business, to change the lives of

other people. And whether the changes we
have made will be, in the end, for good or for
bad, is our look out.'

He thought a moment – then went on in
a quieter, sadder voice: 'I would like to con-
tinue my voyages and my natural history
work, and I would like to go back to Puddleby – as much as any of you. This is
March, and the crocuses will be showing in
the lawn. . . . But that which I feared has
come true: I cannot close my eyes to what
might happen if I should leave these people
and run away. They would probably go back
to their old habits and customs: wars,
superstitions, devil worship, and what not;
and many of the new things we have taught
them might be put to improper use and
make their condition, then, worse by far
than that in which we found them. . . . They
like me, they trust me; they have come to
look to me for help in all their problems and
troubles. And no man wants to do unfair
things to them who trust him. . . . And then
again, *I* like *them*. They are, as it were, my
children – I never had any children of my
own – and I am terribly interested in how
they will grow up. Don't you see what I
mean? How can I possibly run away and

leave them in the lurch? . . . No. I have thought it over a good deal and tried to decide what was best. And I am afraid that the work I took up when I assumed the crown I must stick to. I'm afraid I've got to stay.'

'For good – for your whole life?' asked Bumpo in a low voice.

For some moments the Doctor, frowning, made no answer.

'I don't know,' he said at last. 'Anyhow, for the present there is certainly no hope of my leaving. It wouldn't be right.'

The sad silence that followed was broken finally by a knock upon the door.

With a patient sigh the Doctor got up and put on his crown and cloak again.

'Come in,' he called, sitting down in his chair once more.

The door opened and a footman – one of the hundred and forty-three who were always on night duty – stood bowing in the entrance

'Oh Kindly One,' said he, 'there is a traveller at the palace gate who would have speech with Your Majesty.'

'Another baby's been born, I'll bet a shilling,' muttered Polynesia.

'Did you ask the traveller's name?' inquired the Doctor.

'Yes, Your Majesty,' said the footman. 'It is Long Arrow, the son of Golden Arrow.'

Chapter Three
LONG ARROW'S SCIENCE

'**L**ONG ARROW!' cried the Doctor. 'How splendid! Show him in – show him in at once.'

'I'm so glad,' he continued, turning to us as soon as the footman had gone. 'I've missed Long Arrow terribly. He's an awfully good man to have around – even if he doesn't talk much. Let me see: it's five months now since he went off to Brazil. I'm so glad he's back safe. He does take such tremendous chances with that canoe of his – clever as he is. It's no joke, crossing a hundred miles of open sea in a twelve-foot canoe. I wouldn't care to try it.'

Another knock, and when the door swung open in answer to the Doctor's call, there stood our big friend on the threshold, a smile upon his strong, bronzed face. Behind him appeared two porters carrying loads done up in Indian palm matting. These, when the first salutations were over, Long Arrow ordered to lay their burdens down.

'Behold, oh Kindly One,' said he, 'I bring you, as I promised, my collection of plants that I had hidden in a cave in the Andes. These treasures represent the labours of my life.'

The packages were opened, and inside were many smaller packages and bundles. Carefully they were laid out in rows upon the table.

It appeared at first a large but disappointing display. There were plants, flowers, fruits, leaves, roots, nuts, beans, honeys, gums, bark, seeds, bees, and a few kinds of insects.

The study of plants – or botany, as it is called – was a kind of natural history that had never interested me very much. I had considered it, compared with the study of animals, a dull science. But as Long Arrow began taking up the various things in his collection and explaining their qualities to us, I became more and more fascinated. And before he had done, I was completely absorbed

by the wonders of the Vegetable Kingdom
that he had brought so far.

'These,' said he, taking up a little packet of
big seeds, 'are what I have called
"laughing-beans".'

'What are they for?' asked Bumpo.

'To cause mirth,' said the Indian.

Bumpo, while Long Arrow's back was
turned, took three of the beans and
swallowed them.

'Alas!' said the Indian when he discovered
what Bumpo had done. 'If he wished to try
the powers of these seeds he should have
eaten no more than a quarter of one. Let us
hope that he does not die of laughter.'

The beans' effect upon Bumpo was most
extraordinary. First he broke into a broad
smile; then he began to giggle; finally he
burst into such prolonged roars of hearty
laughter that we had to carry him into the
next room and put him to bed. The Doctor
said afterwards that he probably would
have died laughing if he had not had such a
strong constitution. All through the night
he gurgled happily in his sleep. And even
when we woke him up the next morning he
rolled out of bed still chuckling.

Returning to the Reception Rooms, we

were shown some red roots that Long Arrow told us had the property, when made into a soup with sugar and salt, of causing people to dance with extraordinary speed and endurance. He asked us to try them but we refused, thanking him. After Bumpo's exhibition we were a little afraid of any more experiments for the present.

There was no end to the curious and useful things that Long Arrow had collected: an oil from a vine that would make hair grow in one night; an orange as big as a pumpkin that he had raised in his own mountain garden in Peru; a black honey (he had brought the bees that made it too and the seeds of the flowers they fed on) that would put you to sleep, just with a teaspoonful, and make you wake up fresh in the morning; a nut that made the voice beautiful for singing; a waterweed that stopped cuts from bleeding; a moss that cured snakebite; a lichen that prevented seasickness.

The Doctor of course was tremendously interested. Well into the early hours of the morning he was busy going over the articles on the table one by one, listing their names and writing their properties and descriptions into a notebook as Long Arrow dictated.

'There are things here, Stubbins,' he said as he ended, 'which in the hands of skilled druggists will make a vast difference to the medicine and chemistry of the world. I suspect that this sleeping-honey by itself will take the place of half the bad drugs we have had to use so far. Long Arrow has discovered a pharmacopoeia of his own. Miranda was right: he is a great naturalist. His name deserves to be placed beside Linnaeus. Someday I must get all these things to England. But when,' he added sadly. 'Yes, that's the problem: when?'

Chapter Four
THE SEA SERPENT

FOR a long time after that cabinet meeting of which I have just told you we did not ask the Doctor anything further about going home. Life in Spider Monkey Island went forward – month in, month out – busily and pleasantly. The winter with Christmas celebrations, came and went, and summer was with us once again before we knew it.

As time passed the Doctor became more and more taken up with the care of his big family, and the hours he could spare for his natural history work grew fewer and fewer. I knew that he often still thought of his house and garden in Puddleby and of his old plans and ambitions because once in a while we would notice his face grow thoughtful and a little sad, when something reminded him of England or his old life. But he never spoke of these things. And I truly believe he would have spent the remainder of his days on Spider Monkey Island if it hadn't been for an accident – and for Polynesia.

The old parrot had grown very tired of the Indians and she made no secret of it.

'The very idea,' she said to me one day as we were walking on the seashore – 'the idea of the famous John Dolittle spending his valuable life waiting on these people! Why, it's preposterous!'

All that morning we had been watching the Doctor superintend the building of the new theatre in Popsipetel – there was already an opera house and a concert hall – and finally she had got so grouchy and annoyed at the sight that I had suggested her taking a walk with me.

'Do you really think,' I asked as we sat down on the sands, 'that he will never go back to Puddleby again?'

'I don't know,' said she. 'At one time I felt sure that the thought of the pets he had left behind at the house would take him home soon. But since Miranda brought him word last August that everything was all right there, that hope's gone. For months and months I've been racking my brains to think up a plan. If we could only hit upon something that would turn his thoughts back to natural history again . . . I mean something big enough to get him really excited . . . we might manage it. But how?' – she shrugged her shoulders in disgust – 'How? . . . When all he thinks of now is paving streets and teaching papooses that twice one is two!'

It was a perfect Popsipetel day, bright and hot, blue and yellow. Drowsily I looked out to sea thinking of my mother and father. I wondered if they were getting anxious over my long absence. Beside me old Polynesia went on grumbling away in low, steady tones, and her words began to mingle and mix with the gentle lapping of the waves upon the shore. It may have been the even murmur of her voice, helped by the soft and balmy air, that lulled me to sleep. I don't know. Anyhow, I presently dreamed that the island had moved again – not floatingly as before, but suddenly, jerkily, as though something enormously powerful had heaved it up from its bed just once and let it down.

How long I slept after that I have no idea.

I was awakened by a gentle pecking on the nose.

'Tommy! Tommy!' It was Polynesia's voice. 'Wake up! Gosh, what a boy, to sleep through an earthquake and never notice it! Tommy, listen: here's our chance now. Wake *up*, for goodness' sake!'

'What's the matter?' I asked, sitting up with a yawn.

'Sh! Look!' whispered Polynesia, pointing out to sea.

Still only half awake, I stared before me with bleary, sleep-laden eyes. And in the shallow water, not more than thirty yards from the shore I saw an enormous pale pink shell. Dome-shaped, it towered up in a graceful rainbow curve to a tremendous height, and around its base the surf broke gently in little waves of white. It could have belonged to the wildest dream.

'What in the world is it?' I asked.

'That,' whispered Polynesia, 'is what sailors for hundreds of years have called the *sea serpent*. I've seen it myself more than once from the decks of ships, at long range, curving in and out of the water. But now that I see it close and still, I very strongly suspect that the sea serpent of history is no other than the great glass sea snail that the fidgit told us of. If that isn't the only fish of its kind in the seven seas, call me a carrion crow — Tommy, we're in luck. Our job is to get the Doctor down here to look at that prize specimen before it moves off to the Deep Hole. If we can, then, trust me, we may leave this blessed island yet. You stay here and keep an eye on it while I go after the Doctor. Don't move or speak — don't even breathe heavy: he might be scared — awful timid things, snails. Just watch him, and I'll be back in two shakes.'

Stealthily creeping up the sands till she could get behind the cover of some bushes before she took to her wings, Polynesia went off in the direction of the town, while I remained alone upon the shore fascinatedly watching this unbelievable monster wallowing in the shallow sea.

It moved very little. From time to time it lifted its head out of the water showing its enormously long neck and horns. Occasionally it would try and draw itself up, the way a snail does when he goes to move, but almost at once it would sink down again as if exhausted. It seemed to me to act as though it were hurt underneath, but the lower part of it, which was below the level of the water, I could not see.

I was still absorbed in watching the great beast when Polynesia returned with the Doctor. They approached so silently and so cautiously that I neither saw nor heard them coming till I found them crouching beside me in the sand.

One sight of the snail changed the Doctor completely. His eyes just sparkled with delight. I had not seen him so thrilled and happy since the time we caught the jabizri beetle when we first landed on the island.

'It is he!' he whispered – 'the great glass sea snail himself . . . not a doubt of it. Polynesia, go down the shore a way and see if you can find any of the porpoises for me. Perhaps they can tell us what the snail is doing here. It's very unusual for him to be in shallow water like this. And Stubbins, you go over to the harbour and bring me a small canoe. But be most careful how you paddle it around into this bay. If the snail should take fright and go out into the deeper water, we may never get a chance to see him again.'

'And don't tell any of the Indians,' Polynesia added in a whisper as I moved to go. 'We must keep this a secret or we'll have a crowd of sightseers around here in five minutes. It's mighty lucky we found the snail in a quiet bay.'

Reaching the harbour, I picked out a small light canoe from among the number that were lying there and without telling anyone what I wanted it for, got in and started to paddle it down the shore.

I was mortally afraid that the snail might have left before I got back. And you can imagine how delighted I was, when I rounded a rocky cape and came in sight of the bay, to find he was still there.

Polynesia, I saw, had got her errand done and returned ahead of me, bringing with her a pair of porpoises. These were already conversing in low tones with John Dolittle. I beached the canoe and went up to listen.

'What I want to know,' the Doctor was saying, 'is how the snail comes to be here. I was given to understand that he usually stayed in the Deep Hole, and that when he did come to the surface it was always in mid-ocean.'

'Oh, didn't you know? . . . Haven't you heard?' the porpoises replied: 'You covered up the Deep Hole when you sank the island. Why, yes, you let it down right on top of the mouth of the Hole – sort of put the lid on, as it were. The fishes that were in it at the time have been trying to get out ever since. The great snail had the worst luck of all: the island nipped him by the tail just as he was leaving the Hole for a quiet evening stroll. And he was held there for six months trying to wriggle himself free. Finally he had to heave the whole island up at one end to get his tail loose. Didn't you feel a sort of an earthquake shock about an hour ago?'

'Yes I did,' said the Doctor. 'It shook down part of the theatre I was building.'

'Well, that was the snail heaving up the island to get out of the Hole,' they said. 'All the other fishes saw their chance and escaped when he raised the lid. It was lucky for them he's so big and strong. But the strain of that terrific heave told on him: he sprained a muscle in his tail and it started swelling rather badly. He wanted some quiet place to rest up, and seeing this soft beach handy he crawled in here.'

'Dear me!' said the Doctor. 'I'm terribly sorry. I suppose I should have given some sort of notice that the island was going to be let down. But, to tell the truth, we didn't know it ourselves; it happened by a kind of accident. Do you imagine the poor fellow is hurt very badly?'

'We're not sure,' said the porpoises, 'because none of us can speak his language. But we swam right around him on our way in here, and he did not seem to be really seriously injured.'

'Can't any of your people speak shellfish?' the Doctor asked.

'Not a word,' said they. 'It's a most frightfully difficult language.'

'Do you think that you might be able to find me some kind of a fish that could?'

'We don't know,' said the porpoises. 'We might try.'

'I should be extremely grateful to you if you would,' said the Doctor. 'There are many important questions I want to ask this snail. . . . And besides, I would like to do my best to cure his tail for him. It's the least I can do. After all, it was my fault, indirectly, that he got hurt.'

'Well, if you wait here,' said the porpoises, 'we'll see what can be done.'

Chapter Five
THE SHELLFISH RIDDLE
SOLVED AT LAST

So Doctor Dolittle with a crown on his head sat down upon the shore like King Knut, and waited. And for a whole hour the porpoises kept going and coming, bringing up different kinds of sea beasts from the deep to see if they could help him.

Many and curious were the creatures they produced. It would seem, however, that there were very few things that spoke shellfish except the shellfish themselves. Still, the porpoises grew a little more hopeful when they discovered a very old sea urchin (a funny, ball-like little fellow with long whiskers all over him) who said he could not speak pure shellfish, but he used to understand starfish – enough to get along – when he was young. This was coming nearer, even if it wasn't anything to go crazy about. Leaving the urchin with us, the porpoises went off once more to hunt up a starfish.

They were not long getting one, for they were quite common in those parts. Then, using the sea urchin as an interpreter, they questioned the starfish. He was a rather stupid sort of creature, but he tried his best to be helpful. And after a little patient examination we found to our delight that he could speak shellfish moderately well.

Feeling quite encouraged, the Doctor and I now got into the canoe; and, with the porpoises, the urchin, and the starfish swimming alongside, we paddled very gently out till we were close under the towering shell of the great snail.

And then began the most curious conversation I have ever witnessed. First the starfish would ask the snail something and whatever answer the snail gave, the starfish would tell it to the sea urchin, the urchin. would tell it to the porpoises and the porpoises would tell it to the Doctor.

In this way we obtained considerable information, mostly about the very ancient history of the Animal Kingdom, but we missed a good many of the finer points in the snail's longer speeches on account of the stupidity of the starfish and all this translating from one language to another.

While the snail was speaking, the Doctor and I put our ears against the wall of his shell and found that we could in this way hear the sound of his voice quite plainly. It was, as the fidgit had described, deep and bell-like. But of course we could not understand a single word he said. However the Doctor was by this time terrifically excited about getting near to learning the language he had sought so long. And presently by making the other fishes repeat over and over again short phrases that the snail used, he began to put words together for himself. You see, he was already familiar with one or two fish languages, and that helped him quite a little. After he had practised for a while like this he leaned over the side of the canoe and, putting his face below the water, tried speaking to the snail directly.

It was hard and difficult work, and hours went by before he got any results. But presently I could tell by the happy look on his face that, little by little, he was succeeding.

The sun was low in the west and the cool evening breeze was beginning to rustle softly through the bamboo groves when the Doctor finally turned from his work and said to me, 'Stubbins, I have persuaded the snail to come in on to the dry part of the beach and let me examine his tail. Will you please go back to the town and tell the workmen to stop working on the theatre for today? Then go on to the palace and get my medicine bag. I think I left it under the throne in the Audience Chamber.'

'And remember,' Polynesia whispered as I turned away, 'not a word to a soul. If you get asked questions, keep your mouth shut. Pretend you have a toothache or something.'

This time when I got back to the shore — with the medicine bag — I found the snail high and dry on the beach. Seeing him at his full length like this, it was easy to understand how old time superstitious sailors had called him the sea serpent. He certainly was a most gigantic and, in his way, a graceful, beautiful creature. John Dolittle was examining a swelling on his tail.

From the bag that I had brought the Doctor took a large bottle of embrocation and began rubbing the sprain. Next he took all the bandages he had in the bag and fastened them end to end. But even like that, they were not long enough to go more than halfway round the enormous tail. The Doctor insisted that he must get the swelling strapped tight, somehow. So he sent me off to the palace once more to get all the sheets from the Royal Linen Closet. These Polynesia and I tore into bandages for him. And at last, after terrific exertions, we got the sprain strapped to his satisfaction.

The snail really seemed to be quite pleased with the attention he had received, and he stretched himself in lazy comfort when the Doctor was done. In this position, when the shell on his back was empty, you could look right through it and see the palm trees on the other side.

'I think one of us had better sit up with him all night,' said the Doctor. 'We might put Bumpo on that duty; he's been napping all day, I know — in the summerhouse. It's a pretty bad sprain, that; and if the snail shouldn't be able to sleep, he'll be happier with someone with him for company. He'll get all right, though — in a few days I should judge. If I wasn't so confoundedly busy I'd sit up with him myself. I wish I could because

I still have a lot of things to talk over with him.'

'But, Doctor,' said Polynesia as we prepared to go back to the town, 'you ought to take a holiday. All kings take holidays once in a while — every one of them. And you haven't taken one since you were crowned, have you now?'

'No,' said the Doctor, 'I suppose that's true.'

'Well, now, I'll tell you what you do,' said she: 'as soon as you get back to the palace you publish a royal proclamation that you are going away for a week into the country for your health. And you're going *without any servants*, you understand — just like a plain person. It's called travelling incognito, when kings go off like that. They all do it. . . . It's the only way they can ever have a good time. Then the week you're away you can spend lolling on the beach back there with the snail. How's that?'

'I'd like to,' said the Doctor. 'It sounds most attractive. But there's that new theatre to be built; none of our carpenters would know how to get those rafters on without me to show them. And then there are the babies: these native mothers need my help.'

'Oh, bother the theatre — and the babies, too,' snapped Polynesia. 'The theatre can wait a week. And as for babies, they never have anything more than colic. How do you suppose babies got along before you came here, for heaven's sake? Take a holiday. . . . You need it.'

Chapter Six
THE LAST CABINET MEETING

FROM the way Polynesia talked, I guessed that this idea of a holiday was part of her plan.

The Doctor made no reply, and we walked on silently towards the town. I could see, nevertheless, that her words had made an impression on him.

After supper he disappeared from the palace without saying where he was going – a thing he had never done before. Of course we all knew where he had gone: back to the beach to sit up with the snail. We were sure of it because he had said nothing to Bumpo about attending to the matter.

As soon as the doors were closed upon the cabinet meeting that night, Polynesia addressed the ministry: 'Look here, you fellows,' said she, 'we've simply got to get the Doctor to take this holiday somehow — unless we're willing to stay on this blessed island for the rest of our lives.'

'But what difference,' Bumpo asked, 'is his taking a holiday going to make?'

Impatiently Polynesia turned upon the Minister of the Interior.

'Don't you see? If he has a clear week to get thoroughly interested in his natural history again — marine stuff, his dream of seeing the floor of the ocean, and all that — there may be some chance of his consenting to leave this pesky place. But while he is here on duty as king he never gets a moment to think of anything outside of the business of government.'

'Yes, that's true. He's far too consententious,' Bumpo agreed.

'And besides,' Polynesia went on, 'his only hope of ever getting away from here would be to escape secretly. He's got to leave while he is holiday-making, incognito — when no one knows where he is or what he's doing but us. If he built a ship big enough to cross the sea in, all the Indians would see it and hear it being built, and they'd ask what it was for. They would interfere. They'd sooner have anything happen than lose the Doctor. Why, I believe if they thought he had any idea of escaping, they would put chains on him.'

'Yes, I really think they would,' I agreed. 'Yet without a ship of some kind I don't know how the Doctor is going to get away, even secretly.'

'Well, I'll tell you,' said Polynesia. 'If we do succeed in making him take this holiday, our next step will be to get the sea snail to promise to take us all in his shell and carry us to the mouth of Puddleby River. If we can once get the snail willing, the temptation will be too much for John Dolittle and he'll come, I know — especially as he'll be able to take those new plants and drugs of Long Arrow's to the English doctors, as well as see the floor of the ocean on the way.'

'How thrilling!' I cried. 'Do you mean the snail could take us under the sea all the way back to Puddleby?'

'Certainly,' said Polynesia. 'A little trip like that is nothing to him. He would crawl along the floor of the ocean and the Doctor could see all the sights. Perfectly simple. Oh, John Dolittle will come all right, if we can only get him to take that holiday —

and if the snail will consent to give us the ride.'

'Golly, I hope he does!' sighed Jip. 'I'm sick of these beastly tropics – they make you feel so lazy and good-for-nothing. And there are no rats or anything here – not that a fellow would have the energy to chase 'em even if there were. My, wouldn't I be glad to see old Puddleby and the garden again! And won't Dab-Dab be glad to have us back!'

'By the end of next month,' said I, 'it will be two whole years since we left England – since we pulled up anchor at Kingsbridge and bumped our way out into the river.'

'And got stuck on the mudbank,' added Chee-Chee in a dreamy, faraway voice.

'Do you remember how all the people waved to us from the river wall?' I asked.

'Yes. And I suppose they've often talked about us in the town since,' said Jip – 'wondering whether we're dead or alive.'

'Cease,' said Bumpo. 'I feel I am about to weep from sediment.'

Chapter Seven
THE DOCTOR'S DECISION

ELL, you can guess how glad we were when the next morning the Doctor, after his all-night conversation with the snail, told us that he had made up his mind to take the holiday. A proclamation was published right away by the Town Crier that His Majesty was going into the country for a seven-day rest, but that during his absence the palace and the government offices would be kept open as usual.

Polynesia was immensely pleased. She at once set quietly to work making arrangements for our departure — taking good care the while that no one should get an inkling of where we were going, what we were taking with us, the hour of our leaving, or which of the palace gates we would go out by.

Cunning old schemer that she was, she forgot nothing. And not even we, who were of the Doctor's party, could imagine what reasons she had for some of her preparations. She took me inside and told me that the one thing I must remember to bring with me was *all* of the Doctor's notebooks. Long Arrow, who was the only Indian let into the secret of our destination, said he would like to come with us as far as the beach to see the great snail, and him Polynesia told to be sure and bring his collection of plants. Bumpo she ordered to carry the Doctor's high hat – carefully hidden under his coat. She sent off nearly all the footmen who were on night duty to do errands in the town, so that there should be as few servants as possible to see us leave. And midnight, the hour when most of the townspeople would be asleep, she finally chose for our departure.

We had to take a week's food supply with us for the royal holiday. So, with our other packages, we were heavy laden when on the stroke of twelve we opened the west door of the palace and stepped cautiously and quietly into the moonlit garden.

'Tiptoe incognito,' whispered Bumpo as we gently closed the heavy doors behind us.

No one had seen us leave.

At the foot of the stone steps leading from the Peacock terrace to the Sunken Rosary, something made me pause and look back at the magnificent palace which we had built in this strange, far-off land. Somehow, I felt it in my bones that we were leaving it tonight never to return again. And I wondered what other kings and ministers would dwell in its splendid halls when we were gone. The air was hot, and everything was deadly still but for the gentle splashing of the tame flamingoes paddling in the lily pond. Suddenly the twinkling lantern of a night watchman appeared around the corner of a cypress hedge. Polynesia plucked at my stocking and, in an impatient whisper, bade me hurry before our flight be discovered.

On our arrival at the beach we found the snail already feeling much better and now able to move his tail without pain.

The porpoises (who are by nature inquisitive creatures) were still hanging about in the offing to see if anything of interest was going to happen. Polynesia, the plotter, while the Doctor was occupied with his new patient, signalled to them and drew them aside for a little private chat.

'The porpoises were still hanging about'

'Now, see here, my friends,' said she speaking low, 'you know how much John Dolittle has done for the animals – given his whole life up to them, one might say. Well, here is your chance to do something for him. Listen, he got made king of this island against his will, see? And now that he has taken the job on, he feels that he can't leave it – thinks the Indians won't be able

to get along without him and all that —
which is nonsense, as you and I very well
know. All right. Then here's the point: if
this snail were only willing to take him and
us — and a little baggage — not very much,
thirty or forty pieces, say — inside his shell
and carry us to England, we feel sure that
the Doctor would go because he's just crazy
to mess about on the floor of the ocean.
What's more, this would be his one and only
chance of escape from the island. Now it is
highly important that the Doctor return to
his own country to carry on his proper work,
which means such a lot to the animals of the
world. So what we want you to do is to tell
the sea urchin to tell the starfish to tell the
snail to take us in his shell and carry us to
the Puddleby River. Is that plain?'

'Quite, quite,' said the porpoises. 'And we
will willingly do our very best to persuade
him, for it is, as you say, a perfect shame for
the great man to be wasting his time here
when he is so much needed by the animals.'

'And don't let the Doctor know what you're
about,' said Polynesia as they started to
move off. 'He might balk if he thought we
had any hand in it. Get the snail to offer on
his own account to take us. See?'

John Dolittle, unaware of anything save the work he was engaged on, was standing knee-deep in the shallow water, helping the snail try out his mended tail to see if it was well enough to travel on. Bumpo and Long Arrow, with Chee-Chee and Jip, were lolling at the foot of a palm a little way up the beach. Polynesia and I now went and joined them.

Half an hour passed.

What success the porpoises had met with, we did not know till suddenly the Doctor left the snail's side and came splashing out to us, quite breathless.

'What *do* you think?' he cried. 'While I was talking to the snail just now he offered, of his own accord, to take us all back to England inside his shell. He says he has got to go on a voyage of discovery anyway, to hunt up a new home, now that the Deep Hole is closed. Said it wouldn't be much out of his way to drop us at Puddleby River, if we cared to come along. . . . Goodness, what a chance! I'd love to go. To examine the floor of the ocean all the way from Brazil to Europe! No one ever did it before. What a glorious trip! . . . Oh, that I had never allowed myself to be made king! Now I must see the chance of a lifetime slip by.'

He turned from us and moved down the sands again to the middle beach, gazing wistfully, longingly out at the snail. There was something peculiarly sad and forlorn about him as he stood there on the lonely, moonlit shore, the crown upon his head, his figure showing sharply black against the glittering sea behind.

Out of the darkness at my elbow Polynesia rose and quietly moved down to his side.

'Now, Doctor,' said she in a soft persuasive voice as though she were talking to a wayward child, 'you know this king business is not your real work in life. These natives will be able to get along without you — not so well as they do with you, of course — but they'll manage — the same as they did before you came. Nobody can say you haven't done your duty by them. It was their fault they made you king. Why not accept the snail's offer, and just drop everything now, and go? The work you'll do, the information you'll carry home, will be of far more value than what you're doing here.'

'Good friend,' said the Doctor turning to her sadly, 'I cannot. They would go back to their old unsanitary ways: bad water, uncooked fish, no drainage, enteric fever, and the rest. . . . No, I must think of their health, their welfare. I began life as a people's doctor: I seem to have come back to it in the end. I cannot desert them. Later, perhaps, something will turn up. But I cannot leave them now.'

'That's where you're wrong, Doctor,' said she. 'Now is when you should go. Nothing will "turn up". The longer you stay, the harder it will be to leave. Go now. Go tonight.'

'What, steal away without even saying good-bye to them! Why, Polynesia, what a thing to suggest!'

'A fat chance they would give you to say good-bye!' snorted Polynesia, growing impatient at last. 'I tell you, Doctor, if you go back to that palace tonight, for good-byes or anything else, you will stay there. Now – this moment – is the time for you to go.'

The truth of the old parrot's words seemed to be striking home, for the Doctor stood silent a minute, thinking.

'But there are the notebooks,' he said presently. 'I would have to go back to fetch them.'

'I have them here, Doctor,' said I, speaking up – 'all of them.'

Again he pondered.

'And Long Arrow's collection,' he said. 'I would have to take that with me also.'

'It is here, Oh Kindly One,' came the Indian's deep voice from the shadow beneath the palm.

'But what about provisions,' asked the Doctor, 'food for the journey?'

'We have a week's supply with us, for our holiday,' said Polynesia – 'that's more than we will need.'

For a third time the Doctor was silent and thoughtful.

'And then there's my hat,' he said fretfully at last. 'That settles it: I'll *have* to go back to the palace. I can't leave without my hat. How could I appear in Puddleby with this crown on my head?'

'Here it is, Doctor,' said Bumpo producing the hat, old, battered, and beloved, from under his coat.

Polynesia had indeed thought of everything.

Yet even now we could see the Doctor was still trying to think up further excuses.

'Oh Kindly One,' said Long Arrow, 'why tempt ill fortune? Your way is clear. Your future and your work beckon you back to

your foreign home beyond the sea. With you
will go also what lore I too have gathered for
mankind – to lands where it will be of wider
use than it can ever be here. I see the glim-
merings of dawn in the eastern heaven. Day
is at hand. Go before your subjects are
abroad. Go before your project is discovered.
For truly I believe that if you go not now you
will linger the remainder of your days a
captive king in Popsipetel.'

Great decisions often take no more than a
moment in the making. Against the now
paling sky I saw the Doctor's figure suddenly stiffen. Slowly he lifted the Sacred
Crown from his head and laid it on the
sands.

And when he spoke his voice was choked
with tears.

'They will find it here,' he murmured,
'when they come to search for me. And they
will know that I have gone. . . . My children,
my poor children! I wonder, will they ever
understand why it was I left them. . . . I
wonder, will they ever understand – and
forgive.'

He took his old hat from Bumpo; then
facing Long Arrow, gripped his outstretched
hand in silence.

'You decide aright, Oh Kindly One,' said the Indian — 'though none will miss and mourn you more than Long Arrow, the son of Golden Arrow. Farewell, and may good fortune ever lead you by the hand!'

It was the first and only time I ever saw the Doctor weep. Without a word to any of us, he turned and moved down the beach into the shallow water of the sea.

The snail humped up its back and made an opening between its shoulders and the edge of its shell. The Doctor clambered up and passed within. We followed him, after handing up the baggage. The opening shut tight with a whistling suction noise.

Then turning in the direction of the east, the great creature began moving smoothly forward, down the slope into the deeper waters.

Just as the swirling dark green surf was closing in above our heads, the big morning sun popped his rim up over the edge of the ocean. And through our transparent walls of pearl we saw the watery world about us suddenly light up with that most wondrously colourful of visions, a daybreak beneath the sea.

* * *

The rest of the story of our homeward voyage is soon told.

Our new quarters we found very satisfactory. Inside the spacious shell, the snail's wide back was extremely comfortable to sit and lounge on – better than a sofa, when you once got accustomed to the damp and clammy feeling of it. He asked us, shortly after we started, if we wouldn't mind taking off our boots, as the hobnails in them hurt his back as we ran excitedly from one side to another to see the different sights.

The motion was not unpleasant, very smooth and even; in fact, but for the landscape passing outside, you would not know, on the level going, that you were moving at all.

I had always thought, for some reason or other, that the bottom of the sea was flat. I found that it was just as irregular and changeful as the surface of the dry land. We climbed over great mountain ranges, with peaks towering above peaks. We threaded our way through dense forests of tall sea plants. We crossed wide empty stretches of sandy mud, like deserts – so vast that you went on for a whole day with nothing ahead of you but a dim horizon. Sometimes the scene was moss-covered rolling country, green and restful to the eye like rich pastures, so that you almost looked to see sheep cropping on these underwater downs. And sometimes the snail would roll us forward inside him like peas, when he suddenly dipped downward to descend into some deep secluded valley with steeply sloping sides.

In these lower levels we often came upon the shadowy shapes of dead ships, wrecked and sunk heaven only knows how many years ago, and passing them we would speak in hushed whispers like children seeing monuments in churches.

Here too, in the deeper, darker waters, monstrous fishes, feeding quietly in caves and hollows would suddenly spring up, alarmed at our approach, and flash away into the gloom with the speed of an arrow. While other bolder ones, all sorts of unearthly shapes and colo__urs, would come right up and peer in at us through the shell.

'I suppose they think we are a sort of sanaquarium,' said Bumpo – 'I'd hate to be a fish.'

It was a thrilling and ever-changing show. The Doctor wrote or sketched incessantly

Before long, we had filled all the blank notebooks we had left. Then we searched our pockets for any odd scraps of paper on which to jot down still more observations. We even went through the used books a second time, writing in between the lines, scribbling all over the covers, back and front.

Our greatest difficulty was getting enough light to see by. In the lower waters it was very dim. On the third day we passed a band of fire eels, a sort of large marine glow-worm, and the Doctor asked the snail to get them to come with us for a way. This they did, swimming alongside, and their light was very helpful, though not brilliant.

How our giant shellfish found his way across that vast and gloomy world was a great puzzle to us. John Dolittle asked him by what means he navigated – how he knew he was on the right road to Puddleby River. And what the snail said in reply got the Doctor so excited that, having no paper left, he tore out the lining of his precious hat and covered it with notes.

By night of course it was impossible to see anything, and during the hours of darkness the snail used to swim instead of crawl.

When he did so he could travel at a terrific speed, just by waggling that long tail of his. This was the reason we completed the trip in so short a time — five and a half days.

The air of our chamber, not having a change in the whole voyage, got very close and stuffy, and for the first two days we all had headaches. But after that we got used to it and didn't mind it in the least.

Early in the afternoon of the sixth day, we noticed we were climbing a long, gentle slope. As we went upward it grew lighter. Finally we saw that the snail had crawled right out of the water altogether and had now come to a dead stop on a long strip of grey sand.

Behind us we saw the surface of the sea rippled by the wind. On our left was the mouth of a river with the tide running out. While in front, the low flat land stretched away into the mist — which prevented one from seeing very far in any direction. A pair of wild ducks with craning necks and whirring wings passed over us and disappeared like shadows, seaward.

As a landscape, it was a great change from the hot, brilliant sunshine of Popsipetel.

With the same whistling suction sound,

the snail made the opening for us to crawl out by. As we stepped down upon the marshy land we noticed that a fine drizzling autumn rain was falling.

'Can this be Merrie England?' asked Bumpo, peering into the fog. 'Doesn't look like any place in particular. Maybe the snail hasn't brought us right after all.'

'Yes,' sighed Polynesia, shaking the rain off her feathers, 'this is England, all right. . . . You can tell it by the beastly climate.'

'Oh, but fellows,' cried Jip, as he sniffed up the air in great gulps, 'it has a *smell* – a good and glorious smell! Excuse me a minute: I see a water rat.'

'Sh! Listen!' said Chee-Chee through teeth that chattered with the cold. 'There's Puddleby church-clock striking four. Why don't we divide up the baggage and get moving. We've got a long way to foot it home across the marshes.'

'Let's hope,' I put in, 'that Dab-Dab has a nice fire burning in the kitchen.'

'I'm sure she will,' said the Doctor as he picked out his old handbag from among the bundles. – 'With this wind from the east she'll need it to keep the animals in the house warm. Come on. Let's hug the riverbank so we don't miss our way in the fog. You know, there's something rather attractive in the bad weather of England – when you've got a kitchen fire to look forward to.... Four o'clock! Come along – we'll just be in nice time for tea.'

AFTERWORD

IT has been some time since the *Doctor Dolittle* books have been published in the United States. While they continued to sell millions of copies in more than a dozen languages around the world, ironically in the United States, where this world-renowned story of the doctor who learned to speak the animal languages was first published, the books have been out of print for more than a decade.

It was, therefore, particularly gratifying when Dell Publishing announced plans to bring back the *Doctor Dolittle* books in the United States. Once more Doctor Dolittle, Tommy Stubbins, Matthew Mugg, and the Doctor's animal family from Puddleby-on-the-Marsh — Polynesia the parrot, Dab-Dab the duck, Jip the dog, Too-Too the owl, Chee-Chee the monkey – will be sharing their adventures with a whole new generation of young readers.

When it was decided to reissue the *Doctor Dolittle* books, we were faced with a challenging opportunity and decision. In some of the books there were certain incidents depicted that, in light of today's sensitivities, were considered by some to be disrespectful to ethnic minorities and, therefore, perhaps inappropriate for today's young reader. In these centenary editions this issue is addressed.

The problem that the editors faced was whether or not to delete or rewrite portions of the *Doctor Dolittle* stories. Publishers rightfully believe that it is their job to publish a writer's work, not to act as censors. Because the author is no longer living, it was impossible to obtain his permission to make changes. The *Doctor Dolittle* stories are, moreover, classics of children's literature, and on principle one can make a strong argument that one should not tamper with the classics.

Yet times have changed. Is it appropriate to reissue the *Doctor Dolittle* books exactly as written and stand on principle at the expense of our obligation to respect the feelings of others? Should future generations of children be denied the opportunity to read the *Doctor Dolittle* stories because of a few minor references in one or two of the books that were never intended by the author to comment on any ethnic group, particularly when the references are not an integral or important part of the story? What should our response be when there is widespread disagreement among well-meaning parents, librarians, and teachers as to the proper action to take?

Book banning or censorship is not an American tradition! To change the original could be interpreted as censorship. Then again, so could a decision to deny children access to an entire series of classics on the basis of isolated passing references. These were the difficulties we faced when trying to decide whether or not to reissue the *Doctor Dolittle* books and, if we did, whether or not it was appropriate to make changes in the original versions.

After much soul-searching the consensus was that changes should be made. The deciding factor was the strong belief that the author himself would have immediately approved of making these alterations. Hugh Lofting would have been appalled at the suggestion that any part of his work could give offence and would have been the first to have made the changes himself. In any case, the alterations are minor enough not to interfere with the style and spirit of the original.

In addition, some of the original illustrations from the book have been deleted and others – also original Hugh Lofting illustrations never before published in book form – have been added.

The message that Hugh Lofting conveyed throughout his work was one of respect for life and the rights of all who share the common destiny of our world. That theme permeates the entire *Doctor Dolittle* series. I would like to acknowledge the following editors whose faith in the literary value of these children's classics was invaluable in the publication of the new editions: Janet Chenery, consulting editor; Olga Fricker, Hugh Lofting's sister-in-law, who worked closely with the author and edited the last four original books; Lori Mack, associate editor at Dell; and Lois Myller, whose special love for Doctor Dolittle helped make this project possible. If our alterations help to refocus Hugh Lofting's intended lessons for his young audience, we will know our decision was the right one.

CHRISTOPHER LOFTING

ABOUT THE AUTHOR

HUGH LOFTING was born in Maidenhead, England, in 1886 and was educated at home with his brothers and sister until he was eight. He studied engineering in London and at the Massachusetts Institute of Technology. After his marriage in 1912 he settled in the United States.

During World War One he left his job as a civil engineer, was commissioned a lieutenant in the Irish Guards, and found that writing illustrated letters to his children eased the strain of war. 'There seemed to be very little to write to youngsters from the front; the news was either too horrible or too dull. One thing that kept forcing itself more and more upon my attention was the very considerable part the animals were playing in the war. That was the beginning of an idea: an eccentric country physician with a bent for natural history and a great love of pets. . . .'

These letters became *The Story of Doctor Dolittle,* published in 1920. Children all over the world have read this book and the eleven that followed, for they have been translated into almost every language. *The Voyages of Doctor Dolittle* won the Newbery Medal in 1923. Drawing from the twelve *Doctor Dolittle* volumes, Hugh Lofting's sister-in-law, Olga Fricker, later compiled *Doctor Dolittle: A Treasury.*

Hugh Lofting died in 1947 at his home in Topanga, California.